How the town of S... Montana, came to...

In the 1800s, when William Malone went off to the city to sell a string of mustangs, he also had hopes of enticing folks to come back with him to help build a new town on the Montana plains where there was talk of the railroad going through. He left his young wife, Addie Malone, and their children in the log cabin he'd built just beyond a ridge, where the grass flowed like a carpet of green and a creek bubbled along a stand of cottonwoods. On the day he returned home—bringing four other families with him—he found his young wife standing on the ridge behind their cabin, a shotgun held in her hands, and five thieves lying wounded beyond the ridge. Impressed with her strength and bravery, they had their first town meeting right then and there and named their new town Shotgun Ridge.

With those roots, there was no way the old folks were going to let the population dwindle. The only way to do that was to round up prospective brides and get the local bachelors hitched—pronto!

Be on the lookout for some high-handed matchmaking, as Harlequin American Romance presents BACHELORS OF SHOTGUN RIDGE. Look for more titles in the following months.

Dear Reader,

When I came up with the idea for this cowboy trilogy, I knew these rugged, handsome bachelors would be the main focus. But in creating the little town of Shotgun Ridge, Montana—a town that owed its origins to a brave, strong young woman, Addie Malone, who'd defended her home against thieves with a single repeating shotgun and a fierce determination to protect her family and homestead—I knew I had to create equally as strong heroines for these men, women who would do Addie proud.

It was a woman who saved this town once, and with the help—or meddling, perhaps—of four well-meaning old matchmakers, it will be women who save it now. But convincing these perfectly happy, commitment-shy bachelor cowboys to say "I do" is going to take some doing.

I hope you'll come along with me as these determined heroines attempt to claim the love of three very special, yet stubborn, BACHELORS OF SHOTGUN RIDGE, Wyatt, Ethan and Stony, in: *The Rancher's Mail-Order Bride* (6/00), *The Playboy's Own Miss Prim* (7/00) and *The Horseman's Convenient Wife* (8/00).

I love to hear from readers! Please write to me at: PMB 262, P.O. Box 2704, Huntington Beach, CA 92647.

Warmest regards,

Mindy Neff

The Rancher's Mail-Order Bride

MINDY NEFF

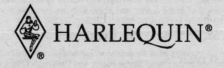

HARLEQUIN®

TORONTO • NEW YORK • LONDON
AMSTERDAM • PARIS • SYDNEY • HAMBURG
STOCKHOLM • ATHENS • TOKYO • MILAN • MADRID
PRAGUE • WARSAW • BUDAPEST • AUCKLAND

To my sister-in-law, Donna Goodger, whose faith,
generosity and goodness I admire so much!

ISBN 0-373-16830-6

THE RANCHER'S MAIL-ORDER BRIDE

Visit us at www.eHarlequin.com

Printed in U.S.A.

ABOUT THE AUTHOR

Originally from Louisiana, Mindy Neff settled in Southern California where she married a really romantic guy and raised five great kids. Family, friends, writing and reading are her passions. When not writing, Mindy's ideal getaway is a good book, hot sunshine and a chair at the river's edge with water lapping at her toes.

Books by Mindy Neff

HARLEQUIN AMERICAN ROMANCE

Don't miss any of our special offers. Write to us at the following address for information on our newest releases.

Harlequin Reader Service
U.S.: 3010 Walden Ave., P.O. Box 1325, Buffalo, NY 14269
Canadian: P.O. Box 609, Fort Erie, Ont. L2A 5X3

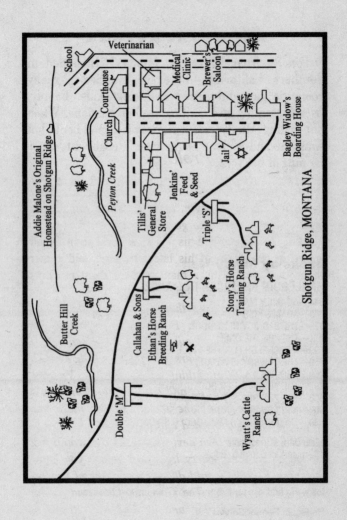

Shotgun Ridge, MONTANA

School

Veterinarian

Church

Courthouse

Medical Clinic

Brewer's Saloon

Addie Malone's Original Homestead on Shotgun Ridge

Peyton Creek

Tillis' General Store

Jenkins' Feed & Seed

Jail

Bagley Widow's Boarding House

Butter Hill Creek

Callahan & Sons
Ethan's Horse Breeding Ranch

Triple 'S'

Stony's Horse Training Ranch

Double 'M'

Wyatt's Cattle Ranch

Prologue

Well, it's about to begin, and I've gotta hope there won't be no shootin' to go along with it.

Ozzie Peyton tapped his pen against his journal and gazed at the photo of his late wife that held center stage over the fireplace mantel where most ranchers hung animal heads and prize antlers.

I'm the one that done the writin' seeing as I'm the romantic in the bunch. Plus, my sweet wife, Vanessa—God rest her soul—was a schoolteacher. I didn't spend all them years helping her grade English papers and not learn a thing or two. Besides, Vanessa taught nearly every boy and man in this town. She'd approve of the plan; she'd want to see these fine young fellows get hitched and have babies.

But left to their own devices, those boys would just go on about their merry lives and before you know it, Shotgun Ridge would die out from lack of procreating! It's not right. The Good Lord started us out with a dang good plan and by dog, the citizens of Shotgun Ridge have abused the whole thing! We've all grown old and our offspring have moved on.

And here we find ourselves in a town full of men.

And those men seem to have forgotten that they have a God-given responsibility to the future of mankind.

Well, me and Lloyd and Henry and Vern have cooked up just the thing to set these cowboys to rights. We all agreed that what we need are women and babies. The gettin' part was just a little tricky.

Especially when it comes to makin' decisions. Like I said, I done the writin'—and I don't for a minute consider any of it lies—but we all, me and Lloyd and Vern and Henry, did the deciding. (And Vanessa had a say in it too, but I don't like to go on to folks about how Vanessa and me still talk. They'd think I was touched in the head or something).

Anyway, what we decided was to put a picture in the magazines and run a couple of ads in the big-city papers to let the women know that we got an unbalanced situation here.

Now, I imagine young Wyatt Malone might be a bit surprised to find that his good-lookin' mug was flashed in the fancy magazines, but the boys and me, we figured he'll get over it. Why it's plain as the nose on a man's face that Wyatt's got a hole in his heart the size of a canyon and it needs healin'.

The thing is, I gotta wonder if we made the right decision when we picked out our candidate from the mail we got. Course it's a little late for second thoughts seeing as how she's due to show up tonight.

Ozzie paused and flexed his hand, working the kinks out of his old joints. He gazed at Vanessa's portrait, gaining strength from her beautiful, soft eyes. Nodding, he licked the tip of his ballpoint pen.

I've known Wyatt Malone all his life, and the boy's as fair-minded as they come. And that's a pretty good thing seeing as how Miss Hannah might be a bit of a surprise....

Chapter One

Hannah Richmond touched the crystal pendant at her neck. The necklace had been a gift from her Aunt Shirley. Hannah had visited her aunt's farm often as a young girl, visits that had created powerful, poignant memories that were etched for a lifetime.

To Hannah, the necklace was a symbol of what she desperately wanted for herself and her children—life on a ranch, a slower pace, love that was genuine. It was an ideal that had grown in her mind to near obsession, an ideal that had compelled her to drive from California to Shotgun Ridge, Montana to start a new life.

To be Wyatt Malone's mail-order bride.

She still went into near hyperventilation about every fifteen minutes—each time she allowed herself to think about her nerve and the enormity of the step she'd actually taken.

She put her hand on Ian's shoulder, gave a reassuring squeeze, both for herself and her son. Just four years old and too often he felt like he had to be a little man. Having a father abandon you tended to do that. And it wasn't fair.

She shivered beneath her lightweight sweater, but didn't want to go back to the truck to get a coat. She might chicken out and keep right on going.

No, she told herself, she wouldn't. This was her ultimate dream and she intended to grab it with both hands. But she sure hadn't realized that springtime in Montana would be this cold!

Taking a breath, she pushed through the door of Brewer's Saloon and paused, scanning the interior. The smell of beer, cooking grease, onions and sweet cigar smoke swirled around her. A sign over the bar admonished patrons to watch their language, that this was a family establishment. She smiled, eased a bit even though butterflies still knocked against her solar plexus, stealing her breath.

The place was more restaurant than saloon, its name misleading. Booths lined two walls. Tables draped in red-and-white-checked cloths were scattered in no particular formation across the plank floor. Through chest-high, swinging saloon doors, a separate room housed a jukebox that played a Faith Hill ballad as cowboys unwound over competitive games of pool.

How was she going to find him?

"Mommy?"

"Yes, Ian?"

"Do we get to eat now?"

"Soon, champ." She'd been traveling in wide-open country for what felt like hundreds of miles, and she hadn't passed a single fast-food restaurant. She was heartened to see that this saloon was indeed an eating establishment. Not that it had been all that long since they'd last eaten, but Ian seemed to be a bottomless pit lately. Probably the boredom of being cooped up in the truck.

She was debating whether to order first and search later when she spotted him. Her heart lurched. Just like it did every time she looked at his picture.

He was standing by one of the booths, smiling and talking with a woman dressed in western wear who looked to be around forty. It was hard to tell.

But Hannah knew the man was Wyatt Malone.

Her cowboy.

She recognized him from the magazine picture she'd carried around with her—the one now tucked inside her purse. She'd memorized this man's features, placed her hopes and dreams on him even though they'd never met.

This was a man whose handwriting she'd traced a hundred times, but whose voice she'd never heard.

With Ian clutching the back of her broomstick skirt, playing peekaboo with the customers in the booths and tables they passed, she made her way across the room.

"Wyatt Malone?"

He turned, did a double take. "Yes?"

Her heart fluttered again. It had been a while since a man had done a double take, given her a quick distracted pass then let his gaze slam back. It did her tattered ego good.

And it gave her hope. It let her know that the physical attraction was mutual.

A person could build on physical attraction. She was banking on it.

"I'm Hannah Richardson?" She hadn't meant to make it a question, for heaven's sake. She sounded like she didn't even know her own self. Which could actually have some validity given the huge chance she'd taken by coming here.

He grinned and tipped back his buff-colored Stetson. "Pleased to meet you. This is Cherry Payne," he said, nodding to the woman who stood by his side. "My neighbor."

Cherry held out her hand and Hannah took it. "Nice to meet you," Cherry said, though there was reserve in her voice. "You're new in town."

"Yes." She sensed the other woman expected more information, but Hannah wasn't used to having intimate conversations with strangers. At least not about why she was "new in town." She was still getting used to the idea herself.

Cherry shrugged and looked back at Wyatt. "I'll leave you be for now. Call me tomorrow and we'll talk about that bull."

"Sure thing." His tone was distracted, apparently because of where his gaze had just landed...and froze.

Hannah lifted her chin and deliberately rested her arm on the shelf of her pregnant stomach. She'd *told* him about the baby, and about Ian. So why did he look so surprised? As though he'd never heard her name or hadn't the slightest idea what she was doing here.

She felt conspicuous and out of place with a room full of cowboys watching her, and an incredibly handsome one standing right in front of her, his eyes kind, yet full of questions.

Fight or flight signals sent adrenaline pounding through her veins, making her dizzy. Her lips felt stiff and shaky with the effort she made at keeping her features pleasant.

Then, Ian peeked out from behind her skirt. "Boo!"

Wyatt leaped back doing a credible job of acting scared, which sent Ian into a gale of giggles. Watching him, Hannah realized that despite his pretense, he looked like he'd truly had a jolt. Then his cheeks creased and he smiled. "Hey, there, partner. Where'd you come from?"

"California," Ian said and hopped up in the booth. "Are you a w-wa-weal cowboy?"

Hannah made a grab for Ian, who'd already clutched a handful of pretzels and was stuffing them in his mouth. "Slow down buddy." His stuttering had improved considerably in the past few months, but he still bobbled his words when he was excited or unsure.

"Yeah, I'm a real cowboy." Wyatt took off his hat and brushed it against his thigh. "Have a seat," he said to Hannah.

"I'm here about the ad?" *Well, duh, Hannah. Great opening line.* She slid into the booth, shifting the bowl of pretzels out of Ian's reach. Why did she keep making her statements sound like questions?

His features cleared to one of recognition, as though he'd finally found himself on solid ground after somebody had given him a rude push. "Ah, yes, the stud."

"Excuse me?"

"The bull."

"No, the bride." She handed him the ad she'd already extracted from her purse.

She was getting a bad feeling here. Wyatt Malone had gone red in the face. And deadly quiet. He held the magazine ad and stared at it as though he'd just awakened from a coma.

That bad feeling inside Hannah grew. "Has there been a change? Mr. Peyton said—"

His head jerked up. "Ozzie?"

"Yes. I wrote to him first and he assured me the ad was legitimate. But he told you that, right?"

Wyatt opened his mouth to answer, but an older man with steel-gray hair and piercing blue eyes rushed over to their table.

"Hannah Richmond," he said, taking her hand and holding it between both of his. "And this must be young Ian. Welcome to Shotgun Ridge. I'm Ozzie Peyton, remember me? We wrote…uh, that first time."

"I remember." But apparently, Wyatt didn't. He was still looking shell-shocked. "I think there's been a mistake, though," she said softly, holding Wyatt's gaze with hers, her eyes as well as her tone asking a question.

"Nonsense," Ozzie said, dismissing her statement with a wave of his age-spotted hand. "You're just feelin' a bit awkward and overwhelmed is all, right Wyatt?"

"I imagine that's the case." His words were slow and deep, his steady gaze unreadable.

"Good. I'll let you two get acquainted." Ozzie fairly ran from the table.

Wyatt smiled, though it felt wooden. He had that sick-in-the-gut feeling as though he'd just been mounted on the meanest bronc in the state and been bucked into the next county.

Ozzie Peyton had some explaining to do.

"Would you excuse me for a minute, Hannah?" He got up from the booth. Keeping his smile in place, he tried to act nonchalant. For the life of him, he couldn't figure out why he didn't just tell her how confused he was, that he'd never seen this ad before in his life.

A color advertisement for a mail-order bride.

The photo was definitely of him, there was no mistaking that. Taken at his ranch, with his hat on his head, a bandanna around his neck, gloves held in one hand, arm propped on the corral fence, booted legs crossed at the ankle, his horse, Tornado, bumping a nose against his shoulder. In the background was the verdant expanse of the Montana prairie and endless blue sky that made the state famous.

"Flag down Maedean and order yourself and Ian a burger. They're messy and greasy, but the best in the county. I'll be right back."

With the ad clutched in his hand, he strode across the room at an agitated clip, his boots scuffing against the scarred plank floor.

Ozzie Peyton stood behind the bar with Lloyd Brewer, the owner of the saloon. He had to give the old geezer credit for not hightailing it out of there when he saw Wyatt coming.

Leaning his elbows on the bar, trying to keep his voice even and reasonable, he said, "What the heck is wrong with you, Ozzie Peyton?"

"Now don't go getting your teat in a wringer, Wyatt."

"*You're* going to have more than that in a wringer if you don't start explaining. That woman over there apparently thinks she's here to be my bride. And from what I've gathered so far, she got that impression from *you.*"

"Well, maybe at first. The rest she sort of thinks she got from you."

"Me?"

"We wrote to her."

"Who's we?"

"Me and Lloyd and Vern and Henry."

The four geriatric musketeers of Shotgun Ridge. God help them all. "Why?"

"Because it ain't right, that's why," Ozzie said in a stage whisper that drew the attention of several of the cowboys bellied up to the bar.

Great, Wyatt thought. Make the spectacle public. He glanced over his shoulder, noticed that Maedean was doing more chatting than order taking with Hannah Richmond.

Double great. The waitress would have Hannah's life history in a matter of seconds and the rest of the town would know it five minutes hence.

Projecting fast forward, he saw events playing out in one of two ways. Either his neighbors would rib him for advertising for a woman—or string him up if he turned her away and caused her sorrow. Never mind that not a soul in town knew the first thing about Hannah Richmond.

The men of Shotgun Ridge were sticklers over how men should treat women, be they sister, mama...or a pretty lady who had the innocent eyes of a fawn and the lips of a siren.

A potent, dangerous combination.

He took a deep breath and tried counting to ten. It didn't work. It still felt as though his life had just slipped out of control like a flatbed hay baler without brakes. "What's not right, Ozzie?"

"The way all you boys around here have ignored your duty. It's a crime against the good Lord, I'm telling you. Shotgun Ridge is dying out. That's why we put the ads in the papers, you bet."

"Ads? My, God, are there more coming?"

"Not for you, so calm down."

"I'm going to pretend I didn't hear that." A man would have to be dead to be calm in a situation like this.

"We ran ads in the papers inviting women to come to town. The ad in the fancy magazine with your picture was the only one for a bride."

His ego reared up in fine form. "And only one woman responded?" Not that he cared he told himself. He wasn't going along with this nonsense.

"Of course not," Ozzie said, giving him a look that suggested he wasn't overly bright. "But me and the boys screened them all and—"

"You screened them? Not very well, apparently.

Ozzie, in case you hadn't noticed, Hannah Richmond has a kid and she's in the family way again!''

"I know that, Wyatt. And I'm surprised to hear you take that tone. You're the least judgmental man I know."

"I'm not judging anybody."

"That's a fine thing to hear. Because the way we see it, this town's in a mess and it's high time somebody did something to rectify matters. There's too much concentratin' on breedin' cows and horses and not enough on breedin' young 'uns!''

"So you brought Hannah Richmond here to have her baby." Well, that wasn't too bad, he thought, relaxing some. Perhaps he'd misunderstood. Perhaps they just wanted her to have her baby here and increase the population.

"And other babies…providing the two of you suit that is.''

Tension shot his spine rigid once more, the image of that insinuation punching Wyatt in the gut. Even after all these years, the pain was still raw. He dismissed it, looked at Ozzie, tried like heck to stand his ground. "Other—?"

"You bet." The old man nodded his head. "We've got an unbalanced situation with a town full of bachelors.''

"Oh, now Ozzie, you're exaggerating. You make it sound like there are no females in Shotgun Ridge when there surely are. One of them comes out to clean my house twice a month. And Miz Parnel over at the beauty shop does a good enough business.''

"How do you know?''

"My mom patronizes Arletta's shop, so obviously the doors are still open for female business—"

"And did she run right home and tell you there were young, eligible women getting permanents and hair dyes?"

"No—"

"I rest my case."

Wyatt could taste frustration in the back of his throat. Communicating with Ozzie Peyton often felt like trying to herd a bull backward through a squeeze chute. "Why would my mother come home and tell me about the customers at the beauty shop?"

"She's a mother wanting grandbabies in her lifetime. That'd make her a natural matchmaker. She'd a told you."

He started to snap that Mary Malone *had* a grandchild. Just because his son was resting in the family plot didn't make him any less of a Malone family member.

But Wyatt didn't have the energy to bring up the argument. Apparently, he had bigger problems on his hands.

"So, since Mom's in Florida, you four old guys are matchmaking?"

"After a fashion, you bet."

Wyatt ran his hand down his face. "And you've corresponded with that woman over there and led her to believe I've invited her here to be my bride?"

"That about sums it up, you bet."

Tonight, Ozzie's distinct habit of tacking on "you bet" to his sentences grated on Wyatt more than usual. "And she's expecting to go home with me?"

Ozzie nodded.

Wyatt turned his full attention to Lloyd Brewer who was watching him in silence, polishing the same glass he'd started on five minutes ago. He was about to rub the shine off it.

"You're in on this Lloyd?" he asked quietly. "My own father-in-law?"

"Becky and Timmy are gone, Wyatt."

Wyatt's jaw tightened and his stomach churned. "I think about that just about every day, Lloyd. I don't need the reminder." When he saw the older man wince, he regretted his tone. Lloyd had taken his daughter's death hard. Still—and because of that—he was surprised that Lloyd would be a party to trying to marry him off to another woman. A stranger.

"It's time to get on with your life, Wyatt."

His fist tightened around the coated paper printed with his picture. "I'm happy with my life just the way it is."

Ozzie and Lloyd gave him a pitying look.

He ignored it. "You all said it before. We're a town of bachelors. Why me?"

"We took a vote," Ozzie admitted uneasily. "It was between you and Ethan Callahan and Stony Stratton."

"Just the three of us?" His tone held a bite but he couldn't help it. This was absurd. "What about the sheriff and the doc? They're young and single. For that matter, so's the preacher. And Ethan's brothers."

"It's a done deal, Wyatt…well, sort of." Ozzie glanced across the room at Hannah. "Give her a chance. Get to know her and see what happens."

"Nothing's going to happen, and you both know it. I had my chance at family and lost it." He looked at Lloyd, then at Ozzie. "Now I just have to figure out how badly you've messed with Hannah Richmond's life and how to let her down easy."

"Don't make too hasty a decision, Wyatt."

He stood, smiled at Hannah who was now looking at him with uneasy questions in her pretty green eyes. Maedean was on her way back to the kitchen, obviously armed with Hannah's order and plenty more....

Like enough information on mail-order brides to entertain the entire population of Shotgun Ridge.

"Bring me one of those messy cheeseburgers, would you, Maedean?" he called, his voice raised above the Friday night crowd and the music.

"You got it, honey." She gave him a bawdy wink.

He sent the gesture back as though nothing in the world was amiss, as though a pregnant woman and little boy weren't waiting for him to come back and jerk the rug right out from under them.

The jukebox was belting out a Shania Twain tune admonishing folks not to be stupid, and two older couples were doing a cowboy waltz across the floor. Glancing around the room, Wyatt realized that what Ozzie said was pretty much true. The men outnumbered the women five to one. Why hadn't he noticed that before? Because he hadn't been interested. Since Becky and Timmy's deaths, he'd concentrated on his ranch and his friends and parents.

Still, a lack of young women was no excuse for the old geezers to run a crazy advertisement in a magazine.

And neglect to tell the beef on the hoof—*him*—about it.

He slid into the booth opposite her. "Did you put in your order?"

"Yes, thanks."

Ian crawled under the table and climbed up on Wyatt's lap.

"Are we g-ga-gonna be your family?"

Wyatt felt as though somebody had reached a fist into his chest and squeezed his heart. The boy was looking at him with solemn eyes filled with hope. No kid this little should hold that much seriousness in his eyes. Before Wyatt could answer, though, Hannah spoke.

"Ian, honey. Remember, we said we'd see?" She looked at Wyatt. "I know my agreeing to come here takes you off the market, but I do want to be cautious."

Off the market? As far as he'd known, he hadn't been *on* the market to begin with. He was beginning to feel a real affinity with his cattle.

"Uh, being cautious is always smart," he said, and nearly swallowed his Adam's apple when Ian's head pressed against his shoulder, little boy breath puffing against his neck.

Maedean came back to the table bearing red plastic baskets filled with steaming French fries and paper-wrapped cheeseburgers. Ian lifted his head to have a look.

"There you go, hon," Maedean said, cupping Ian's cheeks with grandmotherly affection. She frowned, and pressed the backs of her fingers to his forehead. "This little guy's feeling a bit warm."

Hannah was out of the booth and reaching for her son before Maedean had even finished the last syllable. With one knee braced against the vinyl seat right at Wyatt's hip, she steadied herself with a hand on his shoulder, then checked for heat in her son's face.

Her full breasts were aligned perfectly at mouth level; she smelled like a sun-drenched orange grove.

Wyatt's appetite went right over the top, and it wasn't for cheeseburgers.

"Oh, you are hot. Come to Momma, sweetie."

Well, sure. He jerked, cutting off the thought and felt his ears heat when Hannah Richmond gave him a frowning look. Thoroughly disgusted with himself, he concluded he'd been out on the ranch for too long and had completely forgotten his manners. Never mind that the breach was only in his mind.

"Want me to rustle up a thermometer?" Maedean asked. "We could put it under his arm and get a quick reading."

"I think he'll be okay," Hannah said. "But thank you, Maedean."

Wyatt knew they were discussing the boy's fever, but for the life of him, his overactive mind was placing other connotations on the conversation.

"No thanks, needed, hon. You holler if you change your mind, hear?"

Maedean left to attend to the other customers, and Wyatt leaned back, feeling it prudent to put an inch or so of distance between himself and temptation.

When Hannah tried to lift Ian from his arms, he shook his head.

"Sit. I'll hand him to you. He's probably too heavy for you in your condition."

"I'm fine."

She didn't look all that fine. When he finally got his randy thoughts under control, he noticed that her peaches-and-cream complexion was pale with exhaustion, her green eyes weary.

There was a wholesome innocence to her that he normally wouldn't have associated with a woman her age—close to thirty, he'd guess.

He hated like crazy to tell her she had to turn around and go home, that there had been a terrible mistake, but it would be the kindest thing.

Attempting to stand, he was thwarted by the tightening of Ian's arms around his neck. The boy did feel warm. And the smell of French fries didn't seem to tempt. That right there was a sure sign of a kid feeling poorly.

"Don't you want to go sit with your mom, partner? Have something to eat?"

Ian ran his fingers over Wyatt's chin. The rasp of whiskers reminded him that he hadn't gone to a lot of extra grooming trouble before coming to town. Then again, he hadn't expected to be confronted with a bride and a family all rolled into one neat package.

But whether or not he'd shaved was the least of his troublesome thoughts.

"Are you g-gonna be my daddy?"

"Ian!"

Trust a little kid to get right to the heart of matters,

and give him the perfect opening to admit that there had been a mistake fostered by four old matchmaking geezers.

But for some darn reason, he couldn't make the words he needed to say come out. Sticky fingers poked at his Adam's apple and a hard head clipped him in the chin. Fever or not, the kid still had energy to spare.

Hannah Richmond was looking at him with both embarrassment and fragile hope.

Ah, hell. Pregnant with a kid. And apparently prepared to put her future in his hands.

"Why don't we get you home and in a warm bed?" he answered Ian instead, feeling his insides go still at the relief that came over Hannah's soft features.

Relief and a flare of something else he was half afraid to speculate on.

It had been a long time since a woman had gazed at him like he was her salvation, her knight in shining armor. He didn't know why in the world she would do so.

But his ego was just rusty enough to respond, his soul desperate enough to believe.

Chapter Two

"Where did you park your car?" he asked, still a little surprised he was actually going to take this woman and her son home with him.

"It's around the corner, and it's probably got a ticket on the windshield by now. There weren't any parking spaces that looked big enough and I'm not the greatest at maneuvering a trailer around, so I pulled it into a dirt lot down the way."

He shook his head, distracted. "You won't have a ticket. The sheriff's in the saloon."

She smiled, twisted her hands. "That's a relief. I'd hate to start off on the wrong foot."

"You said a trailer?"

She frowned. "It's still okay for me to put my stuff in your barn, isn't it?"

Man alive, he was feeling more and more like he'd walked into the middle of a mystery and was lost in a maze. But he'd already committed himself to taking her home.

"Okay, why don't we leave Ian here with Maedean and the rest of the old boys while we go get your rig.

No sense in him hiking through town if he's running a fever or coming down with something.''

"I don't know. Are you sure…?''

"He's safe here, Hannah. I know every person in this saloon and I'd trust them with my life—and your son's.'' Plus he needed some fresh air and a few minutes alone with her to get his bearings as well as a better idea of what was going on here.

She turned to her son. ''What do you say, Ian? Can you stay here for a few minutes while Wyatt and I go get the truck?''

Ian went still and looked at his mom, suddenly appearing much older than Wyatt imagined he was. "You b-be okay, mom?''

"Sure, pal. You go hop up on that bar stool over there and I'll be right back for you.''

Lightning quick, a smile wreathed the little boy's mouth and he skipped away as though he hadn't a care in the world. Warm cheeks, whether or not they signaled a fever, wouldn't keep him down.

"Sometimes I think my son is four going on forty.''

Four years old. A year younger than Timmy would have been.

Asking Maedean to wrap up the burgers to go, Wyatt put his hand on Hannah's shoulder and led her outside. His pickup was parked in the diagonal space right in front of Brewer's Saloon. Trucks took up most every other parking space on Main Street. No wonder she'd had to park a block away. It was Friday night, and the town—such as it was—was jumping.

They crossed the street and started down the sidewalk in front of the darkened storefronts. He saw her shiver and he took off his jacket and draped it around her shoulders.

She jolted, glanced up at him. "Thank you."

Surprise filled her eyes and her tone. The lady obviously wasn't used to gallantry.

He wondered about her husband—surely it was an ex. Or was the man dead? That was something she'd have more than likely put in her letters.

If he'd done the writing instead of Ozzie, that's certainly one of the main questions he would have asked of an applicant for a wife.

Hell.

He didn't understand why he was so reluctant to tell her that he hadn't run the ad or written any letters. For some reason he couldn't define—just a gut feeling, the kind of feeling he got when something wasn't right with his herd—he didn't want to hurt this woman. He didn't want to burst her dream.

And he didn't even know what her dream was.

But man alive, he liked the way she smelled—like a tangy spray of springtime citrus.

And he had no business noticing or getting attached to her scent or anything else.

He wasn't keeping her. He was only going to be neighborly. After all, she'd driven halfway across the country on good faith. And although he hadn't known a thing about it, he felt responsible.

He spotted the single-axle trailer attached to the S.U.V. in the dirt lot beside the bank. It was bigger than he'd expected; about the size of a horse trailer. It would hold quite a few possessions.

She must have sensed his unease.

"Wyatt. If you've changed your mind, it's okay. We all do things on the spur of the moment, make decisions we end up rethinking in a saner frame of mind."

"Is that what you did? Acted on the spur of the moment?"

"Answering your ad? Yes, I suppose I did. I never expected you to write back. I answered on a lark, and I was sure when you read that I was divorced and had a four-year-old son and was five months pregnant to boot you'd just laugh and toss away my letter."

She'd just handed him some of the information he was tiptoeing around. "So, what did you think when you got a letter back?"

"That it was destiny."

She said it so quickly, so earnestly, he smiled. "Folks out in California put a lot of store in karma and fate and such, right?"

She glanced up at him as though she'd forgotten he was there. "You're making fun."

"No. Really. Just wondering what would make you travel across five states to start over this way."

She fiddled with her necklace, running the crystal pendant back and forth against the gold chain. "I'm tired of the rat race. I want a sense of community, family, a better place to raise my kids."

"Shotgun Ridge's a good place to raise kids—or it was at one time. I hadn't realized until it was recently pointed out, but we seem to have had a crop of boys—and they've all grown up. Most of 'em about my age, I guess."

"Yes. I saw the other ad—the one below yours that said, well…that women and babies were needed."

Wyatt imagined that if they'd had decent lighting he'd have seen her blushing. "So the old geezers in town seem to think."

"I thought you thought it, too."

He kept forgetting he was supposed to have been the one to run the ad. For a bride.

He saw her pass a hand over her stomach and realized he was burning to ask a lot more questions. He wanted to know what kind of man divorced a woman when she was pregnant.

Instead of prying, he steered the conversation back to the town and her reasons for wanting to be here.

"We're a small town—I've lived here all my life and there's definitely that sense of community you were speaking about, though it might not be like the picture you've painted. My closest neighbor is five miles down the road from me."

"That'll actually be refreshing. At home, I can hear the neighbors flush their toilet."

"Surely not." He was astonished.

"With the windows open, yes. I'm tired of feeling as though I'm in the middle of a cement parking lot. I want atmosphere."

"You'll definitely get that here." Though not necessarily with him. He didn't want it to be with him. He'd fallen in love once, and all that he'd held closest to his heart had been snatched away from him in a horrible instant. Much like that destiny thing Hannah had spoken of.

The hurt was too fierce to ever allow himself to go through that kind of trauma again.

Still, the woman had come a long way. She at least deserved a warm bed and a chance to relax, to re-group. He had a sprawling six-bedroom house with only himself to ramble around in since his folks had left.

"If you'll give me the keys, I'll pull the truck around. We'll pick up Ian and I'll drive you back to the ranch."

"What about your truck?"

"Someone will bring it out to me."

"Won't that be an inconvenience? I mean won't you need it?"

He shrugged. "I've got others."

"Still, I can drive myself. Follow you."

He didn't know why he felt so responsible and pro-tective toward this woman, but he did. He shook his head. "The roads are dark and they aren't marked. As long as you're coming out to my place, I'd just as soon make certain you get there whole. And my mama taught me to be chivalrous to the ladies," he added with a smile. She was studying him in a man-ner that made him squirm. Quietly. Thoroughly. Her thoughts carefully masked behind a stillness that made him long to cup her face between his hands and kiss the daylights out of her.

And that thought scared the daylights out of *him*.

She put a hand on his arm. "We can take this really slow—or not at all if that's what you want, Wyatt. I don't want you to feel like you have to accept Ian and me just because we've made the trip."

He frowned, felt the warmth of her palm through the sleeve of his shirt. It surprised him that his heart was slamming against his ribs. "You have some-where else to go?"

Her gaze skittered away. "My sister lives in Bil-lings. She also works for the magazine that you ad-vertised in. She's in Alaska on an assignment for the next month. What I'm trying to say is, if you've had a change of heart, I'll understand. We can use the time we've given ourselves to see if this is really what we want. Or else I can just be a working boarder. In either case, I need a place to stay for a month. At least until Tori gets back from Alaska."

A month.

Why not? He'd do as much for just about any stranger who showed up needing a roof over his head.

And it didn't look like any of the cowboys in Brewer's Saloon were going to offer to take Hannah Richmond and her kid and a half off his hands. Oddly enough, he didn't like the idea that one of them would.

IAN WAS SOUND ASLEEP by the time they reached Wy-att's ranch.

Her new home.

Hannah's heart pounded and her palms were damp. Of course that could have been from the fright she'd suffered when the deer had nearly darted in front of them on the road. Even now, she was having trouble getting her breath back.

"You doing okay over there?" Wyatt asked.

She liked the sound of his voice—soft, smooth and

masculine. He was the epitome of what she'd expected a cowboy to sound like.

And she was getting way too fanciful, she reminded herself.

"Where I'm from, we don't actually play chicken with the wildlife."

He shut off the engine and opened the door. The dome light illuminated his sexy grin and Hannah's heart stumbled all over again. She had to gain some sort of control.

"A deer can do more damage than a freeway pileup."

"You're kidding."

He shook his head. "Usually, by the time you see them, it's too late to do anything. Boom. And hauling a trailer, the last thing you want is to go into a skid. That gets ugly."

"I never thought I'd consider anything good about the California freeways. I think I'll still reserve judgment, though." If she had her way, she wouldn't be going back.

"Welcome to the Double M." He came around and opened her door, holding out his hand to help her down.

For a long moment, she stared at his outstretched hand. She'd been getting in and out of her truck unassisted for as long as she could remember.

That giddy feeling increased. Gentlemanly behavior. She'd forgotten that was still practiced.

She put her hand in his, tried not to let her excitement show. His palm was rough and callused. A workingman's hand.

A hand that could very well hold her dreams in its palm.

She saw the spark of attraction, desire. Okay, so far the plan appeared good. He returned her interest. That meant deeper feelings could grow. She knew enough of human nature to be able to tell if he hated her on sight or if she turned him off.

Neither was the case. And this was a good thing. Very scary, but very good.

"Thank you." All too soon, he let go and Hannah quickly turned away so she wouldn't cling.

It was so dark out. Porch lights shone from the house and another building off to the right, but without the beam of the truck's headlights, that was all she could see.

Millions of stars twinkled in a sky that seemed to go on forever. The crisp night air smelled of animals and earth. No exhaust fumes or smog or hot oil from the corner fast-food place.

The silence was profound, pressing in on her. She was used to traffic and helicopters overhead. Here, there was only the night, the man and the occasional low of an animal.

A dog's soft "woof" brought her attention toward the barn—or was it a stable? She didn't know.

"Oh, isn't he a cutie?" She longed to reach out to the animal, but realized she'd actually backed closer to Wyatt, the side of her body bumping up against his.

"That's Bandit." He clicked his fingers and the dog immediately sat, his tongue lolling, his tail wagging against the dirt. Two dark circles ringed his eyes like a mask. "He's as gentle as they come and loves kids. Spoiled rotten, too."

He said it casually, but she knew he'd picked up on her unease. She liked his sensitivity. With each positive point in his favor, she started to relax, to truly believe that she'd done the right thing by trekking across several states to be some stranger's mail order bride.

"Ian will be in heaven." She reached out a tentative hand and Bandit licked joyfully. That instant jolt of caution flashed through her body and it took more effort than she liked to keep from jerking back her hand. She hadn't been around animals, had never even owned a dog.

She lectured herself to have a spine for heaven's sake. Ranch life was as much about animals as it was land, people and family. And she wasn't going to fail in the first five minutes at something she wanted so badly.

"Why don't you point out which cases you need for tonight. I'll get Ian inside then come back for the luggage."

"I can get Ian."

His gaze lowered to her stomach. "No need. Like I said before, I imagine he's getting pretty heavy for you." He reached inside the truck and unbuckled the seat belt, lifting the little boy out, putting a blanket over him.

"I can at least carry one of the suitcases."

"Leave them. I'll come back."

She wasn't used to this treatment. Or this bossiness. And she wasn't quite sure how she felt about it.

But she followed him to the house and up on the porch. He opened the door without the aid of a key.

At home, she had to struggle with locks as well as dead bolts. Of course here, they were out in the middle of nowhere. It had taken a good fifteen minutes from the main road just to get to the house.

And what a house it was. Sprawling in a squared-off horseshoe shape, two stories, it seemed to go on forever. The front hall had a wood floor accented with rugs to give it warmth. Straight ahead, a massive living room dominated the main floor, with hallways leading off in both directions as well as a staircase. She followed Wyatt up the stairs.

"Sorry about the mess. I wasn't..."

Her hand trailing on the oak banister, she glanced at him. "Wasn't what?"

Wyatt cleared his throat, and lowered his voice. He'd nearly told her he wasn't expecting company, when she clearly thought he was.

The house probably looked like a wreck to Hannah. Newspapers and magazines were strewn on the coffee table and bits of dried mud dusted the pine floor, tracking a path from the kitchen to the wool carpet runner on the stairs.

Cleaning day wasn't until the weekend—and only then if time permitted. And he had no idea if the sheets on the extra beds were clean, or even who'd slept in them last.

"I wasn't sure how it would look to you. It's kind of masculine, I guess."

"Oh, no, it looks very nice."

"I've got a woman from town who comes in twice a month to clean. This is her off week."

"And who does your cooking?"

"I do. At least I have been since my folks bought a motorhome and decided to spend their golden years traveling." He flipped the light switch in the extra bedroom—Timmy's old room. A wave of sadness washed over him.

The nursery furniture had long since been removed—Wyatt's mother's doing. She'd kept a juvenile decor, though: twin beds, dark-blue spreads with quilts folded at the end, a box of toys in the closet for when his cousin, Sheila, visited with her boys. Which they hadn't done for a while. Not since his folks had been traveling.

He wondered if Mary Malone would come rushing home if she found out about the four musketeers' matchmaking scheme. Hell, he was thirty-five years old, for crying out loud. He didn't need his mother to stick up for him. He ran a successful cattle ranch and could take care of himself just fine.

And if he *was* in the market for a bride, he wouldn't need to advertise for one.

"He'll be okay in the single bed, won't he? I mean he won't fall out?"

"He'll be fine. We both will."

"I wasn't going to put you in here with him."

"Oh, I don't mind for now." She ducked her head and he saw her cheeks heat.

For now. She meant until they were married.

Until they were sharing a bed.

His body responded just fine to that image, but his

code of morals gave him the strength to rein in the base thoughts.

Man alive, it was going to be some month.

He stepped aside as she bent to remove Ian's tennis shoes. Her citrusy scent teased his nostrils. She'd been traveling, yet she still looked and smelled fresh and warm and womanly.

He backed up. "I'll go bring in your luggage. Your room's right next door."

"Okay. Just grab the blue cases for now. I'll get the rest tomorrow." She looked at him and added. "If you don't mind."

"I don't mind getting the cases. I *do* mind if you get them tomorrow."

She smiled. "I'm tougher than I look."

He returned the smile. "Yeah, well, cater to my ego a bit, would you? Us cowboys like to show off our muscles and our manners."

She laughed. "Thank you, Wyatt."

He nearly ran down the stairs. That wholesome look of innocence was doing crazy things to his libido.

And making him forget that he *hadn't* placed an ad in the magazines for a mail-order bride.

A ROOSTER CROWED before the sun actually came up and Hannah felt her insides tickle with excitement.

Her first day in Montana.

On Wyatt Malone's ranch.

The smell of coffee brewing tapped right into her fantasies. She'd probably watched more *Little House on the Prairie* and *Bonanza* reruns than most people had.

It was that vision she'd carried in her heart. In her dreams.

She opened her eyes and gave a squeal of fright before she could stop herself.

A wolf stared her right in the face.

Diving under the covers, she waited for sharp fangs to sink into her flesh. Heart thundering, she got a grip and peeked out just as her bedroom door flew all the way open.

Great.

"What's wrong?" Wyatt demanded, coming to a halt inside the room, looking around the floors, at the window and at her.

Feeling like a fool, she held the blanket to her chin with one hand and gestured with her free arm, which was out of the covers. "The dog...?" She let the word trail off because she wasn't absolutely certain that's what the animal was.

"Chinook?" Wyatt frowned and patted his jean covered thigh.

As mannerly as the little dog last night had been, this one trotted over to his side and sat, tongue lolling, a goofy expression on his face now that she got a really good look. "Is that animal smiling?"

Wyatt grinned. "He's male. Wouldn't any guy be smiling if he was in a woman's bedroom and she was still in the bed?"

She didn't know how to respond. If she wasn't mistaken, he was flirting with her. And her own flirting skills were terribly rusty.

She gave a nervous laugh. "Since I'm not a man, I wouldn't know. He looks like a wolf."

"He's part wolf, but don't worry. We rarely let him look in the mirror so he doesn't seem to realize what he is."

She smiled at the affectionate way he talked about the dog—as though it understood him. The image of Chinook admiring himself in the mirror tickled her.

"I feel so silly. It's just that I thought I'd met the dog last night." The cute one with the rings around the eyes.

"Brace yourself. There's still another you haven't met."

"You have *three?*"

"More than that, actually. Lady's got herself a couple of pups."

"Oh, Ian's going to be in dog heaven. I just hope the animals are ready for him. Sorry I scared you."

"I thought you'd seen a snake or something."

She'd been all ready to relax, but at the mere mention of snakes, her hair stood on end. "Are they a problem here?" It was pitiful the way her voice squeaked.

"Spring thaw is early this season, and this is the time of year they come out of hibernation."

Swell. "Do they, uh, often get in the house?"

"Not often, but it's not unheard of."

She nodded and swallowed, trying desperately not to show her fear. She felt enough like a ninny. But she absolutely, positively *hated* snakes.

"Well, I'll get out of here so you can get dressed or go back to sleep, whatever you choose."

"I'll be getting up. I'm used to starting my day early."

"Then you'll get along well here. We usually start before sunup. How about your boy? Is he an early riser?"

"Seven-thirty. Like clockwork, summer or winter, whether he goes to bed at dusk or stays up half the night. You can usually set your watch by him." She felt vulnerable lying here in bed with Wyatt Malone watching her.

He had great eyes—eyes that had spoken to her the moment she'd spotted the magazine advertisement. Deep furrows creased his cheeks when he smiled, making her stomach do cartwheels.

If they decided that they suited one another over the next month, he would have every right to watch her in bed. He'd be her husband.

Knowing her sleep shirt was modest enough, she sat up and finger combed her hair back from her face, her hand pausing in midswipe when she noticed the look on Wyatt's face, the utter stillness of his body.

His gaze was focused on her chest.

He backed up, tripped over the dog. "Fine, uh, I'll see you downstairs."

WYATT HAD BACON sizzling in the skillet, a towel wrapped around his wrist to protect his arm from splattering grease, and a hot cup of coffee on the counter beside him.

Used to being alone, he sensed Hannah's presence before she'd said a word. It was as though her femininity permeated the room on a subliminal level.

He turned, caught himself before he let his jaw drop. This woman set him off balance. She wore a pair of overalls that somewhat disguised her pregnant stomach. Her blond hair was in a ponytail. She looked young. And cute. And Wyatt wanted to waste the day just looking at her.

"Coffee?" he asked. He felt as jumpy as a steer at a slaughterhouse, and he had no idea how to initiate the conversation he knew they needed to have.

She shook her head. "I'm trying not to do caffeine with the baby and all."

"Hell…I mean, shoot."

"You don't have to watch your language around me."

Definitely awkward. "Sure I do. You're a woman, right?"

"Last time I checked."

She laughed, and the sound wrapped around him. He wanted to cover her hand where it rested over her pregnant stomach. But he resisted and pulled open several cabinet doors before he found what he was looking for.

"Here're some tea bags. You can wrestle with brewing them. No, wait." He looked at the box. "This stuff probably has caffeine, too."

"It's okay, Wyatt. A little won't hurt me or the baby."

"How do you get awake without caffeine?"

"It was tough at first, but I've adapted."

"I think you'd have to haul me off somewhere if somebody told me I couldn't have coffee."

"I'll be sure and not tell you that, then."

He noticed that she was unobtrusively glancing at the floors and trying to get a look under the table and under the overhang of the cabinets by the baseboards.

"Did you lose something?" He set the bacon on a paper towel to drain and cracked eggs in the skillet.

Her look was full of guilt and chagrin. "Snakes."

He laughed. "There aren't any snakes in the house, Hannah."

"Well, you said it was a possibility."

"Unlikely. Plus, Chinook would let me know if one came in."

She reached a tentative hand out to Chinook. "Good wolf. No nasty snakes in the house."

Chinook gave a happy bark and Hannah jumped.

Wyatt frowned and Hannah apologized. "I know you said you didn't mind a ready-made family and that you'd teach me about ranch life. But I can see you didn't count on me being so green—and such a chicken around even the dogs."

Wyatt scooped eggs and bacon onto plates and set them on the breakfast table. "I guess it surprises me that you'd come all this way wanting to live on a remote ranch if you've never been around animals."

"I've been around them. Just not recently. Or for very long." Determined to be brave, she reached down, trailed her fingers through Chinook's fur and scratched his ears. He licked her wrist and she smiled at the tickle.

"What are you looking for here, Hannah?"

She sat down at the table feeling as though her feet were resting on quicksand. Had she blown it already?

She wanted this cowboy country life-style so bad—

even though it was only a glamorized image she'd carried in her mind, in her fantasies, she knew it was the reality she wanted. Every instinct she possessed told her so.

"This is probably going to sound stupid to you because it's your life. But I want the vegetable garden and the neighbors helping out without expecting payment. I want the ease of acceptance without the need to put on airs. I want the smell of fresh-ground coffee wafting through the house on a cold morning, the scent of wood burning in a fireplace, the sound of cattle and horses and crickets. The wind blowing through the trees and messing up my hair. The smell of earth and clean air and the feel of pine flooring beneath my feet."

And love. She wanted somebody who would truly love her. Not cheat on her or lie to her or take her for granted. Someone who would accept her and cherish her.

And from all she'd heard, read and seen, these ranchers and cowboys were the true-blue type.

Maybe it was a fairy tale. She didn't know. But it was the fairy tale she wanted. And she would know by the end of the month if it could be hers.

Chapter Three

Wyatt just watched her, not speaking for several long moments. Then he pushed his fingers through his hair.

"Well, we've got the pine floors and the coffee and the cows and horses and crickets. We're a bit short on trees, mostly prairie and hills, but they're out there. I don't have a vegetable garden, but I've got the room for one. Takes more work than you'd think, though. The weeding alone would practically be a full-time job. The neighbors will definitely lend a hand without asking for money, but they've got their own spreads to take care of and don't often get by to socialize." At least he didn't make the effort to get involved.

There had been a time when Becky was alive that they'd gone to barbecues and socials and hay rides and played cards or two-stepped to the local band in town.

He didn't want that life-style again. He didn't want to collect memories that would be like razor wire in his gut when he found himself alone again.

"Better eat those eggs before they get cold," he said and sat down.

"You don't have to fix me breakfast. I should be doing that for you."

He forked eggs in his mouth, didn't comment for a minute. It was silly to picture this woman doing things for him. If a man let himself get too used to an idea, it would take root and become an obsession.

He imagined Hannah Richmond could become quite an obsession.

"I've been cooking on my own a lot of years. Most of the time I don't go so elaborate as this morning."

"Oh. You did this in my honor? I'm ashamed. I don't want you to work harder on my behalf. I should be picking up some of your slack. That's one of the reasons you need a wife, right?"

He blinked. Swallowed hard. *Cooking* and *wife* weren't synonymous in his mind. Now *bed* and *wife* was another matter.

He cleared his throat, got up, grabbed the coffee-pot, and refilled his cup.

"You lived in California all your life?"

"Yes."

"So what made you all gung ho on ranch life? You got visions of dude ranches dancing in that pretty head?"

She smiled and shook her head. "I realize ranching's hard work, and I have to admit I've probably glamorized it in my mind and maybe overestimated my courage level, but I assure you, my determination outweighs most of my fears."

"Good trait to possess. So where'd the idealism come from?"

"My aunt and uncle." She touched her necklace,

an unconscious gesture. "When my sister Tori and I were little, we visited Aunt Shirley and Uncle Rob on their farm in Iowa. The memories are like butterfly wings inside my stomach every time I recall those trips and over the years, it's grown stronger. My aunt and uncle were so much in love and totally committed to each other and their family and the land. It was a dedication they passed on to their children, and sure enough, my cousins grew up to marry and have families and farms of their own." That sense of community and love was what Hannah yearned for.

"So what stopped you from going back to Iowa?"

"Aunt Shirley and Uncle Rob are gone now. Ironically they were killed along with my mom and dad in a train accident."

"Sorry. That must have been a really tough loss."

"Yes. And I've lost touch with the cousins. Actually, I'd never thought about looking for work or a home at their place. I hadn't even known I was going to come *here* until you wrote back."

He picked up his plate and put it in a sink full of soapy water.

"What about your husband?"

"Ex-husband," she corrected.

He glanced over his shoulder. "Ex, then. Doesn't he mind that you've taken his kid and a half out of the state?"

She smiled at his reference to the baby in her womb as half a kid. "I don't see how he could mind since he took off for Jamaica with his latest squeeze the minute he found out I was expecting. Divorce papers came a week later."

Wyatt's mouth tightened in displeasure. "Jerk. How could he just walk out on you like that?" Pregnant for crying out loud. This was a time in a woman's life when she should be especially cherished. Not heaped with responsibilities and heartbreak.

"Oh, I think I knew it was coming. We lived at a pace that threatened to give me ulcers. Allan thrived on that speed, the nightlife and the social scene. He was a successful attorney—well connected. He also thrived on variety." She could still remember the parties he'd dragged her to because it was expected of him, or the ones she'd hosted at their home. He never even tried to disguise his flirtations.

"When I told him I was pregnant with this one he called it quits." She placed a hand protectively over her stomach.

"I repeat, he's a jerk."

"You won't get an argument from me."

"What about Ian? Does he ask about his dad? Miss him?"

"He asked at first. But Allan was never really a part of Ian's life. And Ian's an adaptable kid."

Knuckles rapped on the kitchen door. "Come on in," Wyatt hollered.

The door swung open and Cherry Payne walked in, then stopped in her tracks. "Oh," she said, looking at Hannah. "So, you *did* stay the night."

Knowing the grapevine in a town this small had probably worked overtime, Hannah didn't take offense. She felt a little embarrassed that everyone would know that she'd come here as a mail-order bride, but figured she'd get used to it soon enough.

"Yes." She smiled at the other woman, surprised when the gesture wasn't returned.

Instead, Cherry turned to Wyatt. "I hadn't known you intended to *advertise* for a wife."

Wyatt poured another cup of coffee and leaned against the counter, his booted ankles crossed. Cherry had just presented him with a fine opportunity to get this whole mess out in the open, but he couldn't bring himself to do it this way. Not with Cherry as an audience.

Hannah deserved privacy if she was going to have her dreams dashed.

"You're out early, Cherry," he said rather than comment on her question.

Cherry shrugged and thankfully dropped the subject. "I came by to remind you about the section of fence on Butterhill that's down. The herd's straying, and as much as I trust the sturdiness of your stock, we ought to take care of it." She gave him a wink. "I'll be glad to ride out with you and help fix it. After all, it's on my property, too."

"Thanks for the reminder and offer, but I'm tied up today. I'll send one of the boys out to get right on it, though."

Cherry raised her brows, glanced at Hannah, then back. Wyatt knew claiming to be too busy to take care of a problem was nearly unheard of. Having a strange woman as a houseguest was even more out of character.

Cherry shrugged. "Okay. Just thought I'd check. Send whoever you can. You know where I'll be."

With one last unreadable look at Hannah, Cherry let herself out the door.

Hannah took her plate to the sink and rinsed it. "I don't want to be in the way or keep you from your work."

"I'm the boss man. I make the rules."

He said it easily, but there was a thread of tension in the air. Hannah's spirits plummeted. She was already in the way and had somehow managed to upset one of the neighbors. All in less than twenty-four hours.

Great going, Hannah.

That certainly wasn't the plan—or part of the fantasy. In her mind, she and her next-door neighbors would become best of friends, exchanging recipes and gossip, organizing bake sales at the church.

Cherry Payne didn't strike her as the bake sale type, though. Nor did she appear overly friendly.

Then again, she could be wrong. Perhaps she'd caught the woman on a bad day. Or worse…her mind flashed back to the look on Cherry's face when she'd been talking to Wyatt.

"Is Cherry married?"

"Widowed."

"Ah."

"What do you mean, 'ah'?"

"She cares for you."

"Sure she does. We're neighbors."

"As a man, Wyatt."

"Cherry? Nah." Did she? he wondered. "She's got

a bull I'm trying to talk her out of. She's had a rough time financially since Wendell passed on.'' And that gave him a bit of a twinge that he hadn't dropped everything and gone out to fix the fence. Well, he'd make sure Trevor or Glen got to it today.

"I've got a registered herd and I'm thinking about starting another. I can do that with Casanova.''

"Casanova?''

"The bull. Purebred, nice even disposition. The girls love him.''

"The girls?''

He grinned when she continued to parrot everything he said. To her, a city woman, he would probably sound like he was speaking another language. But he didn't mind. Ranching was his life and he loved to talk about it.

"The cows,'' he explained. "Seems Casanova has more charisma and technique than your average stud.'' He liked that pink in her cheeks, the way he could nearly see her mind putting together images.

"Oh.'' She laughed at herself. "I've got a lot to learn.''

The grandfather clock chimed the half hour, and Ian appeared at the kitchen doorway, looking small and unsure, the hem of his pajama bottoms dragging on the floor.

"Hey. Look who's up.'' She should have gone to his room so he wouldn't have to find his way downstairs in a strange place.

His sleepy gaze traveled around the room and his eyes widened, banishing the last of his grogginess and unease.

"Doggie!" he shrieked and skip-hopped right across the room to throw his arms around Chinook's neck.

Hannah made an instinctive move to protect, to admonish, then caught herself. There was no sense in projecting her silly fears onto her son. Besides, Wyatt had told her the wolf was as tame as a pussycat. She had to trust him.

A difficult thing to do for a woman who'd had to rely on herself more often than not. Although she'd been married for six years, she might as well have been a widow for all the help and support Allan had given her.

Chinook gleefully licked Ian's face, eliciting little-boy giggles and Hannah relaxed, smiling at the joy on her son's features.

"Chinook, show some manners," Wyatt said.

Ian giggled more. "S'nook, show some manners," he mimicked.

Wyatt felt a smile tug at his lips. "Sleep good, partner?"

"Yep. C-could S'nook sleep wif me next?"

"I imagine we'll have a hard time stopping him. How about some eggs?"

"Yuck."

"Watching your cholesterol?"

"Yep."

"Cereal then."

Ian nodded and climbed up on a chair, the mention of breakfast tempting him to quit smothering the poor dog. "Wif lots of s-sugar. You g-g-got lots of sugar, Wyatt?"

"I've got sugar, Ian." He ruffled the boy's hair, trying to ignore the tightening in his chest.

Especially when he saw the way Hannah was looking at him. As though he were a hero.

But he wasn't a hero.

He was going to have to tell this sweet woman and her cute kid that he hadn't sent for them. That he couldn't keep them.

But the sun was shining and the kid was obviously feeling better. Surely this little tyke who was so taken by the animals should see a bit of the ranch before he left.

He poured cereal and milk in a bowl, set it in front of Ian and handed Hannah the plastic canister of sugar, figuring she'd want to regulate the amount that went on top of the cereal.

"When Ian's finished eating, why don't you get him dressed and come on outside. I'll give you the nickle tour of the ranch."

"Do we g-get to ride a horse?"

"Not today, partner."

Ian's face fell. Wyatt felt bad. "Well, maybe later, okay? Right now, though, there're a bunch of mama cows in the corral that we have to see to."

"B-ba-baby cows, too?"

Hannah put her hand on Ian's head. "Eat, buddy. We'll ask questions later."

"Yeah, baby cows, too," Wyatt answered anyway. "Plus some big old daddy ones."

"Way, way big up to the sky?"

"Maybe not quite that big, but close."

"'Kay, I'll h-hurry." He tipped up his cereal bowl

and Hannah's hands shot out to protect the crockery. "Ian, we don't slurp," she admonished.

"Yep, I do."

"Yes, but we *mustn't*."

"Oh." He considered that for a moment. "'Kay."

Hannah looked at Wyatt, attempted to convey apologies. "We're working on the manners." Allan had hated it when Ian was less than perfect. And it had annoyed him to listen to a barrage of questions from a four-year-old.

"Nothing wrong with drinking milk out of the cereal bowl, if you ask me. Takes too long to get it all with the spoon."

She smiled. "Don't encourage him. And you don't have to promise him a horseback ride. He doesn't always get everything he wants." Total understatement. And one of the reasons for the stutter, she suspected.

"Every little boy should have a ride on a horse, Hannah." He picked up his hat and jammed it on his head. "I'll be down by the corral or the barn. Come on out when you're ready."

Hannah nodded and watched him go out the back door, Chinook obediently on his heels. His hat nearly scraped the doorjamb and a pair of gloves stuck out of his back pocket.

His jeans were so tight, it was a wonder anything could fit in the pocket to begin with.

And it was entirely too soon to start thinking about the fit of his jeans.

Wasn't it? They hadn't really talked about how this whole mail-order bride thing was going to work other than his agreement to give it a month to see if they suited.

But that timeline wasn't exactly set in stone, she thought, feeling a giddy flutter in her stomach.

There were such things as falling in love at first sight—or at least very soon. Say within a week? It wasn't unheard of. Aunt Shirley had told her she'd fallen for Uncle Rob one week and married him the next and never looked back.

That's what Hannah was hoping and praying was going to happen with her and Wyatt.

Oh, she knew she wasn't any great beauty, but she was better than average—despite what Allan had said. At least her face was. And her body wasn't that terribly bad. Other than the pregnancy, she hadn't put on too much weight. She was soft and cushy, but not flabby. Womanly, was how she'd describe herself.

She'd answered Wyatt's ad because she was physically attracted to his photo. Unwise, perhaps, but there it was. And she'd hoped that attraction would turn out to be mutual.

Judging by the way Wyatt's gaze lingered on her, she believed that it was.

Her heart skipped and her stomach tumbled as she thought about where that attraction would lead. Would they make love before they decided on the wedding date?

Oh, she just didn't know. She wasn't up on the rules of mail-order brides.

She did know that she was in major lust with her husband-to-be.

And halfway in love with him, too.

She took Ian's bowl to the sink and rinsed it.
"Let's go get you dressed, champ. Then we'll check
out our new digs. I hear there are puppies in the
barn."

"Yeah!" Ian sang, hopping like a jumping bean,
racing around the table. "Doggies! And puppies,
too!"

"Slow down, now."

"No. Hurry, mom."

"Okay." She laughed at the happiness on her son's
face. This was good for him. Just what he needed.
She'd made the right decision by coming here. She
had to believe that.

HANNAH HELD TIGHT to Ian's hand as she walked toward the corral. Chickens squawked and scuttled out
of her way. A goat swung his head around, chewing
a hunk of grass, watching her, contemplating butting
her, Hannah was sure. She nearly ran, but thankfully
exercised some restraint, feeling like an idiot for even
thinking the thought.

Quickest way to show her city roots was to run
screaming across the yard with killer chickens and a
goat on her tail.

She giggled and Ian mimicked the sound, causing
her to laugh outright. Oh, it was a beautiful day. And
she was on a ranch. Halfway to her ultimate dream.

Although she wanted to cling, she let go of Ian's
hand giving him a measure of freedom. Still, she
couldn't help saying, "Stay close to me, now."

"'Kay. What's that?" He pointed.

"That's a rooster."

"And chickens!" he shouted, leaping over a dandelion, then doubling back to snatch it out of the ground.

"Yes."

"Do they got eggs?"

"I'm not sure. Maybe."

"Wow, Mom, look at all the c-c-cows!"

"There's certainly a lot of them." All bumping against one another within the confines of a wood corral. "Let's not get too close, okay." The noise level sounded like these animals weren't all that happy about something.

"Aw, Mom."

A couple of men stopped what they were doing and whipped off their hats when Hannah approached. She smiled. "Is Wyatt out here?" Pretty ridiculous question since she didn't see him, but she didn't know what else to do. He'd said he'd be at the corral or the barn. But there were several buildings to choose from—all wood-sided and painted red.

It had been dark when they'd arrived last night and she hadn't known so many buildings were scattered around the property. Almost like a mini town.

"Try the shop." One of the men pointed to a large building with roll-up doors.

"Thanks." She started in that direction, wondering what in the world a shop was, then saw Wyatt wave to her from the door of yet another building.

Goodness, she'd have to arm him with a cell phone just so she could find him.

A horse nickered and Ian nearly pulled her arm out of the socket trying to get her to pick up the pace.

Which was fine with her. The goat was now keeping up with them and Hannah was seriously worried about its intentions. Shouldn't it be on a leash or something?

"Hi, Wyatt!" Ian called and broke lose. Hannah let him go. She nearly forgot her unease of the trailing goat when Wyatt bent and scooped Ian up in his arms, resting him on one strong shoulder.

Her son squealed and beamed. And Hannah's throat ached.

Then Wyatt looked at her—really looked at her—with one of those steady, interested gazes, and the ache moved downward, changing into something entirely different, something quick and fiery in the pit of her stomach.

Closer now, she saw the change come into his eyes, saw amusement as he glanced behind her. "Picked up an admirer on your way?"

Frowning, she looked over her shoulder and had to swallow the surge of panic that swept over her when she saw the goat. Come to think of it, he *was* looking at her like a lovesick...well, a lovesick goat. She laughed, though the nerves still stuck. "I was a little concerned he might be thinking of charging."

Wyatt shook his head. "Hannah, Hannah. I've told you the males on this ranch are pure gentlemen."

She moved a little closer to Wyatt nonetheless. "Chickens, a goat and roosters—it seems more like a farm than a ranch."

"My mom's an animal lover. She'll drag home anything." He set Ian on the ground. "Check out the last stall over there."

Hannah picked her way through the stalls, trying unsuccessfully to keep a rein on Ian who was intent on chasing everything that had fur or feathers attached to it.

"Ian—"

"Let him be. He's fine," Wyatt said.

She wasn't sure about that. Chickens could peck and goats could butt—despite Wyatt's claim that this one was well mannered. And the horses were awfully big. It seemed to her if they got it in their mind to do so, they could escape their stalls with a well-placed kick of a hoof.

She told herself she was going to get this unease under control. It was just that she didn't know about the animals. Once she learned, she wouldn't be such a Nervous Nelly.

She hoped.

Keeping her shoulder out of nipping range of the horse's teeth, she glanced in the last stall and her eyes widened when she came upon a camel-like animal and it's young one. "What in the world?"

"Meet Fancy. Our resident llama."

The llama blinked, looking bored, and continued to chew on hay. Hannah blinked back, then gave a half smothered giggle as something turquoise flashed in the corner of her eye.

Strutting down the middle of the barn as though taking a stroll down Rodeo Drive in Beverly Hills was a beautiful peacock, it's vivid tail feathers dragging on the dirt floor of the barn.

"My goodness, you've got a zoo here."

Wyatt grinned and shrugged. "A lot of mouths to

feed, but what can you do?'' He gave Tornado a scratch between the ears and checked the straw in Dusty's stall. ''The calving shed's over in the next building, but you probably don't want to go there today. The smell's enough to knock you out at times.''

''Calving shed? I thought cows just dropped their babies on their own.'' She *had* done a bit of reading before she'd come.

''Mostly. But first-time moms sometimes have a little trouble. We'll bring them in the shed and put 'em in a jug—a stall—and watch them to make sure they don't need a little help.''

''I'd like a *lot* of help when my time comes, thank you very much.''

His gaze shifted to her stomach. ''Did you have an easy time of it with Ian?''

''Actually, yes. Four hours. This one will probably be even quicker.''

Wyatt frowned. Out on a ranch like this, that could be scary. They weren't exactly around the corner from town or a hospital. He'd hauled Becky to the hospital three times before it was actually the real thing and even then, it had taken thirty-six hours for her to deliver.

The thought of four hours or less was enough to make his palms sweat. It took over an hour just to get to the hospital. And what if she used up the other three thinking her pains were false ones?

His mind automatically started running through options. Chance Hammond didn't mind making house calls, but Wyatt wasn't sure what the doctor's specialty was. Chance's family was from Shotgun Ridge, so after medical school, Chance had come back home to set up a general practice. That had been about three years ago.

Wyatt tried to think back, to remember if any babies had been born. He didn't think so. Which would probably mean that wasn't one of Chance's specialties—if he even did it at all. He'd only used the young doctor a couple times—to set a broken bone when Glen had flipped the four-wheeler, and to treat a nasty infection on Steve's leg courtesy of an angry heifer and a cow pasture full of mud and dung.

Still, Hammond was a doctor. And he could make it out to the ranch in about twenty minutes...

Why was he even thinking about her being here when her time came? She would stay the month until her sister returned home from her assignment. Then she would be on her way.

Even though she made his blood run hot, he had to tell her he wasn't interested in a wife. That he hadn't placed the ad.

Chapter Four

Needing to get his mind back on the tour and off Hannah's labor and delivery, Wyatt tugged at his hat.

"Okay, ready to go see some cows?"

"Yeah!" Ian shouted.

"Didn't you say something earlier about puppies?" Hannah asked instead.

Ian, looking as though he'd been told he could pick any item in a candy store, but only one, danced back and forth, looking from Wyatt to Hannah, then back again.

"We could see c-c-cows *and* puppies," he asked hopefully, trying to hurry the decision along.

"Right you are, partner. We have to go past the cows to get to the puppies. I don't know why Lady decided to have her litter in the shop, but that's where they are."

"Oh," Hannah said. "And the shop is another, uh, barn?"

"It's where we keep all the equipment, the tractors, hay balers, four-wheelers and trucks and stuff."

She looked a little disappointed. "You mean you don't use your horses for your work?"

"Oh, we still ride every chance we get—despite modern technology. In fact, this beauty's mine." He paused beside Tornado's stall again and stroked the horse's neck.

"Me, too!" Ian sang and Wyatt lifted him so he could touch the horse. A bit overexuberant, his little hand streaked out.

Tornado's head jerked, and he bolted.

Hannah jumped.

"Easy," Wyatt soothed, both for the horse's benefit and Hannah's.

She'd automatically backed up a step, shying like the skittish horse. She seemed to catch herself soon enough, and though Wyatt was holding Ian in his arms, he could see her motherly instincts take over as she squared her shoulders and moved back up beside him, placing her hand on her son's thigh.

Wyatt smiled. Hannah Richmond was scared silly of half the animals on this ranch and doing her level best not to show it. He had to give her credit for her spunk and her determination to protect her son despite her fears.

She glared at him when she caught the grin. "Well, I told you in my letter that I didn't know the first thing about animals and you said that was okay."

His grin grew wider. "And so it is."

"With a little time and some instruction, I'll be a pro at ranching and animal care. You wait and see."

That took the grin off his face. She might end up

being a pro at ranching, but it wouldn't be on *his* ranch. It was just plain silly to think otherwise.

He hadn't advertised for a wife, and he wasn't interested in acquiring one. He was perfectly content with his life the way it was.

But that didn't stop him from appreciating this sexy woman who radiated serenity with a hint of flash.

Suddenly the barn seemed too close and intimate. Even over the smell of hay and leather and horses, Hannah's subtle citrus scent teased him, made his thoughts wander and his decent intentions waver.

"Let's go have some bull-vaccinating instruction. We'll start out with the two-thousand-pound variety and from then on, the rest of the critters will be a breeze."

"Poke fun if you must," she said and elbowed him in the side. "I'll be riding in a rodeo by next spring."

"Tough lady." He liked the way she bumped against him, both when she was teasing him or when she was unsure and simply took an instinctive step closer, trusting that he would protect her.

That absolute, blind trust made him feel about ten feet tall.

Again, he had to wonder at the kind of man who could throw this woman and kid away. Her ex-husband was an idiot.

He set Ian on his feet, tickled when both he and Chinook seemed to decide at the same time to torment the goat. With a gleeful shriek and a happy canine bark, boy and dog charged the goat.

"Come back!" Ian admonished the goat.

Looking confused, Chinook sat, tongue lolling, ears

perked as he glanced back and forth between the goat and Ian. Clearly he'd thought they were supposed to give chase, but now he wasn't sure.

Ian fixed it all with an exuberant hug to the dog's neck. "Good S'nook. Nice puppy. B-but don't scare the goat. 'Kay? We gotta be sweet."

Wyatt grinned. There was something about that kid that got to him. And he couldn't explain it.

"I bet you tell him to be sweet a lot."

Hannah laughed. "You can tell, huh?"

"We'll need to find another word. Cowboys are rarely sweet."

"Oh, I don't know about that. You seem to have your moments."

He shouldn't let this easiness between them continue. It wasn't fair to let Hannah get her hopes up. But it felt awfully good to have female companionship. To talk and flirt and feel all macho and capable.

They walked into the sunshine and headed across the yard. Trevor and Steve were urging a bull into the chute when something went wrong. With a thunder of hooves and the loud split of wood, the bull broke through the corral fence and charged across the holding pen, causing a nervous stampede of heifers standing guard over their newly branded and vaccinated calves.

Hannah automatically grabbed for Ian as the commotion started up, cupping his shoulders so he'd stay close. Clouds of red dust billowed and the colorful shouts of cowboys split the air.

Wyatt stepped in front of Hannah and Ian as though he intended to shield them with his body if need be.

Hannah's heart pounded as adrenaline surged. She didn't know whether to run or stand her ground. That bull had broken through one fence, he could just as easily break another and come right at them.

Idiotically, she glanced down at what she and Ian were wearing, thankful their clothes weren't red.

Bulls charged at red, didn't they?

"You two stay back a ways," Wyatt said, his tone short and tight, his lean body already coiled and bunched as he headed for the fray.

He didn't have to tell her twice. She had no intention of getting too close. In fact, she'd about decided she'd had enough instruction and initiation for one day and would just as soon soak up the ambiance of ranch life from the safety of the kitchen.

But watching Wyatt stride purposefully toward a corral full of excited cows, and one terribly upset bull, was a sight she simply couldn't turn away from. Like a crash on a freeway, she had to look.

Not that there was danger, she told herself. Wyatt knew what he was doing.

She sucked in her breath and revised her opinion when he went right through the corral gate, closing himself in with that maniac bull.

"What the heck is going on here, Steve?"

"Sorry, boss. This one's been giving us trouble. I thought he'd settled down and I could get him in the chute."

"You know better than to mess with a bull on the fight like this," Wyatt admonished. The angry animal was glaring balefully. "Everybody just stand back."

Hannah wanted to object. But having known him

for less than twenty-four hours, she didn't feel she had the right.

"We can get him, boss."

Wyatt shook his head. "I said, stand back. It's my ranch and my bull and my responsibility."

The cowboys all got behind the fence. Despite herself, Hannah took a half step closer, her hands still clutching Ian's shoulders.

She watched, frightened, yet excited as Wyatt snatched off his hat, slapped it against his thigh, and took an aggressive step toward the bull. Neither man nor animal looked ready to back down.

Waving the hat like a mighty, gleaming sword, he shouted at the bull. "Go on, now you son of a gun. Move!"

The bull tossed his head and pawed the ground as though he would charge. Hannah held her breath. For once, even Ian was still.

"I said, move!" Wyatt shouted, advancing another step.

"No," Hannah whispered.

One of the cowboys turned to her. "He knows what he's doing, ma'am. Don't worry."

Incredibly enough, the bull gave Wyatt one last irritated look, then trotted out the gate and back into the fenced pathway the other cowboys had been trying to get him into in the first place.

Hannah didn't quite know how to define what she was feeling. Breathless, giddy, fascinated…excited.

Wyatt was a man's man and that was a powerful aphrodisiac. He took charge. Was capable. Showed no fear.

With his buff-colored hat back on his head, he strode toward the gate, boots scuffing in the dust, hips loose, jeans tight and sexy, his button-front long-sleeved shirt molding to his chest.

She thought of Allan, with his soft hands, clean nails and the strong scent of cologne that lingered everywhere he went, permeating the house, the car and his clothes. She recalled how he'd thrown a hissy fit when he'd had a flat tire, hadn't even thought about fixing it himself. Probably because he didn't know how.

The only things Allan knew how to do well were litigate and commit adultery.

Wyatt, on the other hand, was the type of man who lived by a code and would go to the mat for it.

The type of man she desperately wanted.

And if this sexy, competent cowboy could fall in love with her, she'd be the happiest woman on earth.

Her goal now was to make sure that happened. She would be the best thing that ever came along for him. She would show him just what an asset she could be.

Latching the corral fence, Wyatt came up next to Hannah.

"Make a note of that one's number, Trevor," he said, jerking his head toward the ornery bull. "He's history. I don't need that kind of grief or attitude."

"Will do, boss. If you get Cherry Peyton's Casanova, you won't have run-in's like that."

"We'll still have to deal with the rest of the bulls," he reminded, "but I *am* working on getting Casanova. Did you meet Hannah and Ian?"

"We exchanged a word. Pleased to meet you, ma'am," Trevor said and took off his hat.

Hannah wished he wouldn't call her ma'am. It made her feel old. Oh, thirty was far from ancient, but she wanted to think of herself as young, wanted Wyatt to see her that way. To be attracted to her—

"Hannah?" Wyatt was looking at her oddly.

"Oh. Nice to meet you too, Trevor. This is my son, Ian."

"Are you a cowboy, too?" Ian asked.

"Sure am, little buddy."

"I—I'm gonna be a c-cowboy."

"Slow down, Ian," Hannah said softly.

The little boy nodded, clearly embarrassed. Hannah looked heartbroken, as though she wanted desperately to fix her son, but couldn't.

Wyatt reached down and hoisted the boy up to his shoulder, eliciting a shriek and a giggle, all thoughts of stuttering and their causes forgotten for the moment.

"I believe this just about covers the cows and bulls, wouldn't you say?"

Hannah breathed a sigh of relief. "It *is* exciting, I'll give you that."

Wyatt grinned. "Onward to the puppies."

"Yeah!" Ian bucked and kicked like a featherweight bronc rider. "To the puppies!"

OKAY, HANNAH THOUGHT as she armed herself with a bucket full of cleaning supplies. She'd definitely had a trial by fire today. Dogs, chickens, a goat, rooster, horses, cows, angry bulls, a peacock and a llama of all things! A lizard had scuttled by, but that wasn't so bad. She'd coped.

Now snakes were another matter altogether, she thought as she gave the toilet she was about to clean a surreptitious look.

Wyatt had cautioned her to be alert—not scared, but alert. When she'd pinned him down on the matter, he'd mentioned they liked to hide under rocks and in shady places.

In California, she'd heard of snakes getting loose in the sewer system and coming up through the toilet. It was her worse nightmare.

Lord above, she could see the headlines now: "Woman found dead in the bathroom, pants around her knees and no apparent reason for a healthy woman of thirty to suffer a heart attack."

Apparent would be the key word some ingenious sleuth would pick up on, somehow getting to the bottom of the mystery. The new headlines would read: "Snake enters toilet by way of sewer pipes and gooses woman in the bare behind, frightening her—*literally*—to death."

Hannah shuddered and did a little dance. Catching sight of herself in the mirror over the sink, she felt like a fool. An emotion that was beginning to feel second nature.

Get a grip, Hannah. She briskly swished the toilet brush around the bowl, flushed and slammed down the lid. The bathroom was clean enough, she decided.

Anyway, now that she'd been exposed to all the animals, she could systematically learn to get along with them, make peace with them.

Prove to Wyatt Malone that he hadn't chosen wrong when he'd agreed to have her as his mail-order bride.

She'd start with the easy ones—the dogs—and work her way up, perhaps chickens next. Or the goat. That one truly did appear taken with her.

Perhaps some Internet research on the care of goats would be in order. She wondered if Wyatt even had a computer or was hooked up to a local server for Internet access.

With the toilet brush in one hand and the bucket in the other, she came around the upstairs corner and slammed right into Wyatt.

"Oh!" Her breasts tingled and her breath rushed out in a whoosh. The bucket dropped to the floor.

His hands shot out automatically, grabbing her shoulders, then her stomach, his big palms cupping her pregnant belly with a reverence that nearly melted her bones.

"Are you okay? Did I hurt you?"

Nervous, off balance, she said, "I'm fine. Thankfully my chest still sticks out farther than my stomach." The minute the words left her mouth she went scarlet.

And Wyatt's gaze went right to the thirty-four Ds in question.

His lips twitched, his hazel eyes filled with amusement and something much hotter. "Yes. Thankfully." A murmur. Almost a prayer.

"I didn't expect you home so soon. I was just cleaning a bit." This felt so awkward—explaining her actions in his house. It was still so new.

"You don't have to clean."

"Oh, I don't mind. Ian's resting—he had a full and wonderful day with all the animals, but I'm afraid it wore him out. I had some time on my hands and thought I'd make myself useful." And hopefully, indispensable.

"You could have rested with him. You shouldn't overdo things in your condition."

She smiled when he still looked skeptical. "I'm fine Wyatt. I had a check-up right before I came to Montana and I'm taking my pre-natal vitamins religiously." His consideration was so sweet. She was going to have a good life with this sexy cowboy. The thought of it made her giddy.

Provided she could get him to love her, that is.

She glanced at her watch. "I put a roast in the oven, but it's got another hour to go yet. Should I have planned dinner sooner?"

"An hour will be fine. That'll give me a chance to shower. I don't imagine I smell any too pretty."

"You smell fine." She ducked her head. Boy did he smell fine. All male. Cowboy male. Just like her fantasies. But the real thing was so much better.

Her gaze fastened on his chest, broad and strong, then moved up his neck, lingering for a half a second on the red bandanna tied there, then onward to his lips.

Sensual, unsmiling lips that were bracketed by deep creases etched by humor and heredity.

"Hannah."

"Yes?"

"You really shouldn't be looking at me like that."

Feeling pleasantly dazed, her eyes lifted, met his. She licked her lips. "Like what?"

The growl issued from the back of his throat could have been distress or desire. "Like I'm on the dinner menu."

"Sorry." It was a half whisper. She touched his chest, her palm right over his heart. She didn't know where the boldness came from, but it rose up inside her, clamoring for release.

He tensed, and although he didn't back away, she instinctively knew that he wanted to.

Or felt he *had* to.

"I haven't been kissed in over five years." She hadn't known she was going to say that, hadn't known it mattered. But it did. Desperately.

His gaze shot down to her stomach, then back up. "Excuse me?"

"Having sex and getting pregnant doesn't always involve kissing."

"It sure as hell does." He sounded appalled.

She shook her head, slowly, couldn't help but stare at his lips, her own mouth parting. It was as though she was held in some sort of marvelous spell.

"You're serious?"

"Yes. Now that I really think about it. Allan might have given me a few closed-mouth kisses or pecks on the cheek, but I haven't really been kissed in…in way too long. Would you…?"

She never had a chance to finish the request.

He pulled her tight against his chest, their bodies pressed in a way that made her ache and pulse and feel exactly like a woman. His lips were warm and firm and sure. With very little pressure and an abundance of expertise, he traced the seam of her lips with his tongue, asking for and gaining entrance.

Hannah sagged against him and moaned, the sound swallowed in his mouth as he angled her head and took her deeper, farther.

Created genuine magic with just the simple touch of his lips and tongue.

Her heart bumped against her rib cage as desire raced rampant through her body, setting her on fire, awakening long-dormant sensations. She might be five months pregnant, but she hadn't experienced this depth of desire and arousal in years—if ever.

Not only were her nerve endings awakened, but so was the baby in her womb. It kicked, causing Wyatt to jerk back.

He looked about as stunned as she felt.

"Well," she said when she finally had enough breath to do so. "That was worth the wait."

His cheeks actually turned red, charming her.

"Glad to oblige." He cleared his throat. "I better go take that shower now."

Watching him walk away, Hannah touched trembling fingers to her well-kissed lips. If she hadn't been in love with him before, she certainly was now.

Any man who could kiss like that, make her toes curl inside her shoes, was a man to keep.

Why had she ever thought she could settle for less with Allan?

She wondered if she'd been too forward just now. Would he think her a racy woman? Loose and free and easy. Oh, she knew that most people thought of

Californians as faster—with cars, sex, plastic sur-
geons and just about every other decadent thing imag-
inable.

But Hannah wasn't like that.

She had just needed, *badly,* to be kissed.

When Wyatt shut the bathroom door, she twirled,
right there in the upstairs hallway, the forgotten toilet
brush now clutched to her bosom like a bouquet of
cactus blossoms.

Oh, my gosh! She'd just kissed the sexiest cowboy
on the planet while she was holding a toilet brush!
The very thought tickled her.

WYATT WAS STILL having trouble getting his body to
settle down, and that was after half an hour in a cold
shower.

What in the world had possessed him to kiss her
like that? He knew damned well he wasn't keeping
her. So, why had he allowed himself a taste?

A single taste that now felt like it would never be
enough, would haunt him without respite.

The smell of garlic roast filled the kitchen, making
his mouth water. She kissed like a million bucks, and
if the delicious scents in the kitchen were any indi-
cation, she cooked like a dream, too.

But no matter her qualifications, he wasn't looking
for a wife.

So, why the devil had he kissed her? He'd lost his
mind, that was all. It was the innocence in her irides-
cent green eyes, the siren song of her lips, the under-
stated sensuality that made a man willing to walk
across barbed wire just for a taste.

Man, if he kept this up, he was going to need to soak himself in the icy creek. He debated skipping out and going to the bunkhouse with the guys. But he wasn't a coward.

He had to face her.

And he had to come clean about the ad.

When he'd passed her bedroom door a few minutes ago, he'd heard her talking to Ian. The boy had obviously woken from his late nap. Which meant discussions would have to be put off a while longer. He didn't want to get into the whole thing with Ian present. But it would have to be done soon.

He couldn't keep kissing her. Leading her on.

The back door burst open and Skeeter Hawkins walked in. He had the bowlegged gait of a lifelong horseman, and was the best foreman in the county.

"I take a couple of days off to go bury a nephew and what happens? I come back to hear you've gone and advertised for a bride, that's what."

"I didn't advertise for a bride." Skeeter had been working on the Double M since Wyatt was in his teens. The man was practically family. "How's Marilyn?"

"Holdin' up."

"And you?" Skeeter's nephew had been a great pride to the old cowboy. A successful engineer with a fine family who'd been struck with cancer at the indecently young age of thirty-two. Three years younger than Wyatt.

"I'm good. Best thing is to get back to work. Tried to talk Marilyn into coming home with me, but she's wanting to stick close to the grandchildren. Worry's me some with her stiff upper lip and all. Time will tell.'' Skeeter opened the oven door and sniffed.

''Smells pretty dang good. So, why'd you advertise for a mail-order bride?''

''I told you, I didn't.''

A gasp at the kitchen doorway had Wyatt whirling around.

Hannah stood there clutching Ian's hand, her face pale. ''You didn't run that ad?''

Chapter Five

Wyatt could have kicked himself for not keeping his voice down. He hadn't wanted her to find out this way.

Granted, he hadn't figured out how to tell her, but this certainly wasn't it. She needed gentleness. She'd gotten bluntness.

It was inexcusable.

He went to her, started to reach out.

"You didn't place the ad?" she asked again, her voice strained.

"No," he said softly, his heart aching at the emotions chasing across her face, the stunned, hollow-eyed look of disbelief, of shattered hopes.

"But…your picture… Who—?"

"Ozzie and some of the other men in town."

"Why?"

"They have some crazy notion that the town's gonna die—"

"No." Hannah held up her hand. A chill washed through her, followed by the heat of embarrassment. He was looking at her with something that very closely resembled pity. She couldn't abide that. She'd had her fill of patronizing from Allan.

"Why didn't you say something? How could you bring me out here? To your house?" The buzzing in her ears nearly drowned out the thoughts flipping at warp speed through her brain. She had a U-Haul trailer outside, still hooked up to the truck, filled with all her worldly possessions. There wasn't a lot there that held sentimental value—except for the curio cabinet that had been Grandmother O'Malley's. Earlier in the day she'd decided it would go nicely in the front room, between the hallway to the west wing and the dining room.

How presumptuous of her.

He hadn't even advertised for her.

Even worse, she'd kissed him like there was no tomorrow. Practically begged for that kiss! Her mortification went straight through the roof.

"I felt responsible."

"Respons— oh, I'm so embarrassed. I can't believe... I'll get my things right now and be out of here before—"

"No!" Ian cried. "You p-p-pr-promised we c-c-could live on th-th-the ranch!"

Hannah bent down, hugged Ian to her. "Take it easy, sweetheart. Slow down. It's going to be fine."

"There's h-horses here, and *dogs!*" He sobbed against her shoulder.

"I know, buddy."

Wyatt bent down and tapped Ian on the shoulder. The tears broke his heart. "Hey, partner."

When Ian peeked at him, he patted the boy gently

on the back, his fingers brushing against Hannah's. For just a bare instant, his gaze went to hers, noting the utter heartbreak there, too. Heartbreak for her son. Maybe a little bit for herself. He felt like scum.

"There's someone I'd like you to meet."

The little boy's lashes were spiked with tears, his nose running, brown eyes filled with a wariness that no four-year old should know. Wyatt swept a thumb beneath Ian's eye, lingered just a moment over the baby-soft chubby cheeks, the feel creating an ache in his gut that he didn't want to examine.

"Skeeter's about the best cowboy around and knows all about roping cattle. I bet he'd be happy to show you how to twirl a rope."

Ian looked at Skeeter with a spark of cautious interest swimming in his eyes. If only it were always this easy to distract. The resilience of youth should never be battered by the hard knocks of life, but what should be and what *was* didn't always mesh.

"Dang right," Skeeter said. "I'm the ropin' champion. Leastways I was back in '83. What do you say, little buddy? Want to go have a bit of practice with me before we lose all the light and the bugs get to munchin'?"

A fleeting smile nearly tipped Ian's lips. He glanced at Wyatt. For permission. For reassurance.

The responsibility that single look put on Wyatt's shoulders was awesome and humbling. He nodded. "You go. I'll try to fix it in here with your mom, okay?"

"'Kay," Ian said, then went over to Skeeter and slipped his hand into the old cowboy's ham-size paw.

Wyatt waited until they'd gone out the back door before he spoke. "Hopefully Skeeter won't teach him to spit along with the rope lessons."

The attempt to lighten the atmosphere fell flat.

"You shouldn't have told my son you'd fix things. He's had enough empty promises in his life—and those were from a man who was *supposed* to love him. He doesn't need them from a stranger."

That hurt. Never mind that he *was* essentially a stranger. A part of his heart that he normally kept firmly locked had opened a crack. He didn't feel like a stranger. Nor did he want to be.

"Seems to me I'm not the one who took the chance on empty promises." He hadn't meant to bite back like that, winced at the hurt that leaped into her green eyes.

"I had no idea they were empty," she defended. "The letters you wrote to me said this was what you wanted. You..." She closed her eyes. "You didn't write them. My God, I'm so sorry. You must've thought I was some kind of nut."

"No. I didn't think you were a nut. And I'm sorry. I shouldn't have said what I did just now, and I shouldn't have given your son hope. But there's no reason why it can't be, Hannah. Stay for a while. Let him enjoy the animals and the ambiance."

"For a while?"

"Yes." He could tell she was going to turn him down even before she shook her head. Inspiration struck. "You came here for the life-style, Hannah. Not for me."

She opened her mouth, started to say something, then seemed to change her mind. "So?"

"So stay. Let me introduce you around."

"Introduce... Are you suggesting that you'll be my *matchmaker?*"

If Ozzie could, *he* could. "I guess. Sort of."

"Why?"

"Because I feel responsible." He held up a hand, cut her off before she could let pride speak for her. "You packed up your belongings and your kid and crossed five states. And I don't think you did that on a whim."

He saw her touch the necklace, give a self-deprecating roll of her eyes. He wanted to hold her in his arms. He reined in the impulse.

"Making a decision in a short period of time is different than acting on a foolish whim, Hannah. You've thought about this for years, haven't you? You're looking for what your Aunt Shirley had." He had her attention now.

"And you've come to the right place for that. Just not the right man." Even though he believed that with all his heart, it stung to say it, to accept it. Ridiculous.

"All the more reason I should get out of here."

"No. Shotgun Ridge is filled with good, honest, hardworking people. Men. Stay, Hannah. We'll socialize some, introduce you around. You'll have so many suitors, you'll have to beat them off with a stick. We'll find you that husband so you can have your dream and your life on a ranch that you want."

"But not with you." It was a statement, delivered softly, sadly, the hint of embarrassment still there.

He sighed. "No. Not with me. I had my chance at family and lost. I just can't do it again."

Hannah swallowed against the bitter regret that backed up in her throat. The advertisement had said Wyatt was a widower. She'd thought that by placing the ad for another bride, he was over the heartache. "Your wife?" she asked.

"And son."

Her heart did a quick, stinging flop. "Oh, Wyatt. I'm so sorry." To lose a child was the worst devastation, too unbearable to even contemplate. She wanted to know details but his tight body language told her he'd exhausted that particular subject for now.

"So, what do you say? Will you stay? We can start at church tomorrow. Let you meet folks. Take your time. Fall in love face-to-face rather than settle for some out-of-focus picture of an old cowboy who's set in his ways and not likely to change." His eyes telegraphed apology.

She could have told him it was too late to change emotional gears. She'd already fallen in love with her cowboy. Wyatt Malone.

He had a valid point about Ian, though. Her son *had* been uprooted too many times in his young life, both emotionally as well as physically. Perhaps she could go along with Wyatt's crazy plan.

But put a different spin on it.

"You said your sister was in Alaska. At least take the month you'd already settled on. Think of it as a vacation."

Her pride did balk at this. "No—"

He barreled right over her attempted objection. "You don't have to give up your dream. You can practice on my ranch. Even plant a garden. You said you wanted a garden, remember? And I'll teach you about those animals like Ozzie promised you I would."

She found herself smiling. Maybe it wasn't so far-fetched. He seemed to be going out of his way to convince her. Was it all motivated by guilt? And only meant to be short-term?

Or could he actually have a seed of caring for her, a tiny kernel that he couldn't see just yet, but could grow with a little care and nurturing and prodding?

That possibility was what had her nodding her head, agreeing to let him become her matchmaker.

While Wyatt Malone was scoping out suitable cowboys for her to marry, she would do her best to make *him* fall in love with her.

It was a gamble, undoubtedly an uphill battle. But she was up to the task.

She'd crossed five states for this man, and she wasn't going to give him up without a fight—be it fair or otherwise.

HANNAH WAS going to have a serious talk with that rooster. The silly bird couldn't quite seem to figure out when dawn was imminent. He started in around 3:00 a.m. and kept right on crowing, obviously figuring he'd get it right eventually.

Problem was, a person couldn't get a decent night's sleep.

Blurry-eyed, she stumbled down to the kitchen.

She'd kill for a cup of coffee. Never mind about the report she'd read that had advised expectant mothers to go easy on caffeine. The final verdict wasn't in. It was probably a rumor started by some killjoy naturalist or something.

One cup wouldn't hurt, and it would at least get her functioning—which she wasn't at the moment due to that horrible chicken. Maybe they could cook him.

She had the coffee pot in her hand and nearly dropped it when the back door opened.

Wyatt, looking exactly like every one of her cowboy fantasies, walked in and came to a sudden halt as though he'd slammed into a brick wall.

Pot suspended over a mug like a thief caught with her hands on the family silver, she cleared her throat. "It's just one cup," she defended.

His dark brows rose, lifting his hat. Lord that was sexy.

"I didn't say anything." His grin was slow and frankly male. "Get up on the wrong side of the bed?"

"As a matter of fact…how do you feel about a little rifle instruction using that senile rooster as the target?"

"Hannah, Hannah. Such thoughts on a Sunday morning."

She inhaled the rich aroma of strong black coffee, smiled into her cup and sipped, nearly moaning in delight. "Did you make this?"

"Yes."

"It's wonderful." She noted the dirt smudging his cheek and crusting at the knees of his jeans. He looked like he'd been crawling through the mud. "Speaking of Sunday, weren't we going to church?"

"Yes."

"Looks like you've been working."

"I have. Ranching's a seven-day-a-week job. The animals have to be fed, chores seen to."

"Oh." And if she intended to be a rancher's wife, she'd need to know these things, be prepared and able to help out. She considered herself a quick study. "What time do services start?"

"Ten."

"Then I'll get breakfast started."

"You don't have to cook. I told you, you should treat this like a vacation."

"It's not a vacation. It's a way of life that I desperately want. And I'm an excellent cook."

He hesitated. "You'll spoil me and then go off and cook for some other lucky guy."

Not if she could help it. "So enjoy the pampering while it's being offered."

He nodded. "I'll go get cleaned up. Don't run yourself short of time. It takes about half an hour or so to get to the church." He hesitated, took off his hat, ran the brim between his fingers. "We should probably start even earlier than that. Give us a chance to check out the congregation, introduce you around."

Find her a husband.

THE CHURCH WAS just as she'd pictured it. White wood siding, narrow steps leading up to double doors, a steeple reaching toward the endless blue sky, stained glass shining in the morning sun. Budding flowers outlined a verdant lawn of spring grass.

People milled by the front door, shaking hands and slapping one another on the back, no doubt catching up with the latest news from their friends.

A little girl in a sunny-yellow dress and shiny Mary Janes ran toward a tire swing hanging from an old cottonwood tree, but was called back by her father. Looking crestfallen, yet obedient, she turned around, then snagged a happy pansy and stuck it in her mink-colored hair, dancing around her father like a mischievous puppy.

Wyatt opened the truck door and held out a hand to help Hannah down. "Relax," he said. "You look beautiful." The pale-pink sweater skimmed her hips, nearly disguising the pregnancy. She looked fresh and innocent—and she appeared startled by his comment.

She ducked her head. "Thank you."

"What's that look for? Surely you've gotten compliments before?" Changing his mind, he bypassed her hand and lifted her down from the truck, setting her on her feet in front of him.

She sucked in a breath, her gaze slamming to his before skittering away. He'd caught her off guard. Her cheeks took on a charming glow. With that complexion she couldn't hide much.

"I've been married for the past six years and only divorced for four months. I guess compliments are a bit of a novelty."

He stared as though she were speaking a different language and she felt the need to elaborate. "According to my ex, I'd never be skinny enough because my hips are too big.''

''You're joking, right?''

She shook her head.

''A strong wind would blow you away.''

''Oh, now, let's not exaggerate.''

He wasn't. She was voluptuous on top—thanks in part to her pregnancy, he suspected. But her hips were not wide. ''Believe me, I'm not. Those city guys might want to drape an arm over a stick, but around here a man appreciates a woman with curves. It's sexy.'' He reached in the back seat of the truck and unbuckled Ian's seat belt. ''Let's go get preached to, partner.''

''I c-could preach. I go to Sunday school, and we learned verses. But Jimmy ate the stars and frew up, a-and it stinked!''

''Ate the stars?'' Wyatt asked, confused.

''Stickers they get for each Bible verse they learned,'' Hannah said absently, still rehashing and basking in his comment about curves. Some of her curves were sticking out in the wrong directions, but by darn, she was certain Wyatt Malone had just told her she was sexy!

''Ah. Sticker stars.''

''Do they got k-kids here to play wif?'' Ian hopped up and down like he had to pee or something.

Wyatt asked him as much and Ian went into gales of laughter. ''No, silly!''

''Well,'' Wyatt said to Hannah when she grinned at him. ''He looks like he does.''

''He's got a lot of energy.'' Hannah put a hand on

her son's head. "Slow down, buddy. We're here to listen to a sermon, not play." Besides, according to the ad Ozzie had run, women and children were in short supply.

She frowned and squeezed Wyatt's arm. "Did Ozzie run ads for any of the other men in town, or just you?"

"Just me." He lowered his head, the brim of his hat shading his eyes. "At least for the bride thing. Evidently they ran some general invitations for women to come for a visit and plan to stay a while."

"I'm not going to be the only woman here, am I?" She glanced around the churchyard, relieved to see that although men were the majority, there were indeed women.

"No. Those four old musketeers as we like to call them, exaggerated. There are other women here. But they're mostly older, I guess. Or already married."

"The little girl over there looks about Ian's age." Hannah pointed to the one decorating herself with pansies.

"That's Stony Stratton's daughter. Actually, she's his goddaughter who he's raising. And you're right. I think Nikki's about five."

She saw the calculating look that came over Wyatt, and wondered if he was considering Stony as a matchmaking prospect. She didn't comment or encourage.

It hurt that Wyatt was so anxious to get rid of her. Then she thought back to how he'd worked so hard to convince her to stay on his ranch. He hadn't offered to haul her into town and put her up at the local hotel.

That gave her hope. She'd have to play it by ear, watch his reactions as she interacted with the church congregation—especially the males.

That would tell her a lot.

A young man wearing a Western suit and shiny boots came toward them, a wide smile on his handsome face. "Wyatt! Good to see you. And this must be Hannah and Ian."

Did everybody know who she was? Hannah felt the heat of embarrassment scald her face. Would these people think she was some kind of loser, a woman who couldn't get a decent man on her own so she had to resort to mail-order-bride ads?

The man took Hannah's hand in both of his. "I'm Dan Lucas. The guy who prays over most of these sorry cowboys' souls."

"Oh. Pleased to meet you Pastor Lucas." This was a preacher? He didn't look like any man of the cloth that she'd ever seen. He was handsome, early to midthirties, with just enough flirtatiousness in his eyes to make a woman's heart pump a little harder.

She felt Wyatt's sleeve brush her arm and noticed that he was frowning, practically standing on top of her.

"You three go on in and find a seat. But not in the back row," he admonished with a look at Wyatt. "And don't run off after the service. Vera and Iris have fixed up enough chicken and potato salad to feed the entire county. Hannah and Ian are our guests of honor."

"Oh, thank you. You all shouldn't have gone to the trouble."

"What trouble? We'll use just about any excuse to eat and fellowship around here. Plus the ladies like to keep their hand in—a sort of practice for weddings and such." The pastor's eyes gleamed with pure anticipation.

"I'm sure you've got other parishioners to greet," Wyatt said, putting a hand at Hannah's waist and urging her forward. "We'll see you after the sermon."

Pastor Dan laughed. "Pay close attention. We'll be discussing Noah and his part in repopulating the world."

Wyatt ran a hand down his face then paused and peered through his index and middle finger as the preacher gave a wink and a jaunty wave.

Hannah nearly laughed. When they were out of earshot of the preacher, she said, "He was teasing you, right?"

Wyatt shook his head. "I'm not real sure. And I don't know why the heck they decided to pick on me." He glanced down at her. "No offense."

"None taken." She smiled. That spark of possessiveness he'd displayed when the preacher had held her hand gave her a great deal of hope.

And though she felt a bit like she was in the hot seat, that the whole congregation would be speculating over her, she decided that this day just might be interesting and telling.

"Hey, there, California."

Wyatt's brows slammed down. The man standing in front of them with his blond good looks and lady-killer smile was what he imagined most women would consider male perfection. Add in the guy's fortune and he'd be considered a pretty good catch.

Wyatt didn't even consider him in the running.

"Ethan Callahan, meet Hannah Richmond. And quit drooling in her fried chicken, would you?"

Ethan cocked a brow as if to say 'what's up?' and for no good reason, Wyatt wanted to deck him. He heaped more potato salad on his plate instead.

"Welcome to Shotgun Ridge, Hannah. And I assure you, I don't drool."

Hannah laughed and Wyatt scowled even more. Couldn't she see that the guy was nothing more than a playboy, flirt? Despite the fact that Ethan Callahan was one of Wyatt's best friends, he wasn't the right man for Hannah.

Man, this matchmaking thing was going to be more difficult than he'd expected. There were so many factors to consider.

He'd brought her to church to introduce her around, begin the campaign to find her a husband. To do right by her, correct the wrong perpetrated by Ozzie—however well intended.

The problem was, he hadn't counted on his reaction. It almost felt like jealousy, which was absurd. He had no intention of keeping her, of marrying her. Hell, she'd blown into his life, been sprung on him, actually. Nobody in their right mind—Ozzie, Lloyd, Vern, and Henry aside—would expect him to go through with the plan.

A blind date was one thing.

A mail-order bride was quite another.

Still, he couldn't just turn her away when all her

possessions were in a U-Haul trailer and her sister wasn't due back for a month. She wanted life on a ranch. And he wanted to get that for her.

But she'd had a rough time of it, what with her lousy husband stepping out on her and all—and there were still parts of that story that he was highly curious about.

It stood to reason that she'd be vulnerable right now. He didn't want to feel responsible for her making a mistake, getting hooked up to the wrong guy around here.

Besides that, she had a lot to learn about ranching. *He'd* promised to teach her. Granted, Ozzie had technically been the one to agree on his behalf through their letters, but Wyatt had seconded it once light had been shed on the situation.

"You going to turn loose of her, Malone, and let her get to know folks?" Ethan asked. "Or just keep her all to yourself?"

Before he could answer, Hannah gave a soft smile that rendered both Wyatt and Ethan dumb for a split second.

"Actually, if you'll both excuse me, I need to corral Ian before he pulls the tablecloth off in an attempt to make a fort. And I'm going to find who made this potato salad and get the recipe."

"That would be Iris Brewer," Wyatt said. He recognized his mother-in-law's salad. He'd had it twice a month for a lot of years. "Small woman, curly brown hair. She's over there by the coffee."

"Thanks...oh, no. Ian!" She charged off to avert disaster between a fluted platter teetering on the edge of a table as a tablecloth got hooked in Nikki's shoe buckle.

Stony Stratton came to stand beside Wyatt and Ethan, watching the children create mischief. "Think I should get involved?"

"Nah," Wyatt said. Stony was a man of few words, a gentle giant who was the best horse trainer in the country as far as Wyatt was concerned. He could take any animal and work miracles. "They're just feeling their oats a little."

Stony nodded. "Nikki will be glad of the playmate."

"You'll have to let her come out to the ranch," Wyatt said before he thought his words through.

Ethan leaned a shoulder against the wall, slouching in a casual way that managed to look macho and elegant all at once. And Wyatt felt like an idiot noticing the mannerisms of his friends. God help him if they saw him at it.

"So, the rumor's true? You ran an ad for a bride?" Ethan Callahan's tone held just enough amused taunting to grate.

"No. I did not."

Ethan and Stony both raised their brows, but waited for Wyatt to elaborate.

"The four musketeers did it."

"No kidding?" Commiseration replaced amusement.

"They ought to be shot for pulling a stunt like this. Hannah showed up thinking I knew she was coming."

"From California," Ethan said with a nod. "I

heard about it from Cherry. She didn't seem pleased and if you ask me, she might be rethinking the sale of that bull. If that's the case I might put a bid in for old Casanova myself.''

Wyatt felt his blood pressure rise. ''Did she say she'd changed her mind?''

''Not in so many words, but then again, I'm an expert when it comes to reading women. Casanova and me have some things in common. The more I think about it, the better I like the idea of owning that stud.''

''Keep your lady's-man paws off my bull.''

Ethan grinned. ''So, the old guys decided you needed a wife?''

''Pretty much.''

''Lloyd went along, too?'' Stony's quiet tone held surprise.

Wyatt shrugged and nodded at the same time. All three men remained silent for a moment. Ethan and Stony had been pallbearers at Becky and Timmy's funerals. Ethan had been Timmy's godfather. Playboy tendencies aside, Ethan was as loyal and levelheaded as they came. He'd have trusted his friend with Timmy in an instant.

And just remembering that baby boy ripped a hole in Wyatt's gut.

''I don't plan to go through marriage and kids again. You know that. But I feel responsible. Hannah thought I'd written to her.''

''So, what are you going to do?''

He shrugged. ''She's got her heart set on life on a ranch. She's tired of the fast-track living. She was married to a jerk who cheated on her and walked out on her when he got her pregnant the second time.''

Stony and Ethan's features hardened. It was difficult for any of them to imagine a man treating a woman that way.

''I'm telling you, that woman's got some courage,'' Wyatt said, watching as Vera Tillis stopped her to talk. ''And she's had some tough breaks. I don't want to be the one to add to her heartache.''

''But she knows now that you didn't run the ad, doesn't she?'' Ethan asked.

''Yeah. She was embarrassed, and her little kid was devastated. I couldn't let them leave.''

''So maybe something will work out after all.'' Stony commented.

Wyatt shook his head. ''Not with me. But I figured I could introduce her around, find her a decent husband.''

Both Ethan and Stony jerked to attention as though they'd been goosed by a red-hot cattle prod. ''Don't look in my direction,'' Ethan said.

''Get real. I wouldn't let her marry you.''

About to relax, Ethan decided he'd been insulted and should object on principal. ''Why not?''

''Because you've got more looks and money than God and you're a flighty playboy.''

Ethan shrugged, relaxing once more. ''Sounds like some pretty good attributes to me.''

Stony snorted, but kept silent, obviously thinking if he didn't speak he wouldn't become a candidate for husband.

''I'm going to give the matter some careful

thought," Wyatt said. "In the meantime, Hannah and Ian will be staying at my place. Ian's tickled with the animals and Hannah's looking to plant a garden."

"A garden?"

Wyatt ignored the speculative looks on his friends' faces. "It's just a few seeds and some dirt. It's not permanent."

Ethan grinned. "Well, better you than me, buddy."

"Don't get too smug—either of you," Wyatt said. "Ozzie and the guys ran ads in several of the big-city papers inviting women to come on over to Shot-gun Ridge. No telling what they have in store for the two of you." Pleased with the look of horror that crossed their faces, Wyatt tossed his paper plate in the trash barrel.

"There's a piece of chocolate cake over there that's got my name on it. Anybody else want some?"

"Might as well get it before your cowhands hog it all."

Trevor, Steve and Brant were standing around the dessert table. "Looks like they're all a little awestruck with your bride-to-be," Stony commented, his deep voice soft and causal.

"She's not my..." Wyatt followed their line of sight—right to Hannah.

And just as Stony had said, all three of his wranglers were looking like lovesick puppies.

He'd have to nip that right in the bud. Those boys lived on his ranch. Hannah needed a place of her own. He couldn't let her take up residence in the bunk-house, for crying out loud.

And he couldn't stand the thought of her being with another man and him having to see it every day.

That worried him. He shouldn't care. Caring was a dangerous thing. You never knew when the ones you loved would be snatched away. And to care deeply and have that happen was too much to bear.

He knew that better than most.

Chapter Six

Hannah had corralled Ian and Nikki and redirected them to expend their energies outside, thus saving the platter of vegetables and artichoke dip.

She'd been stopped by just about everyone in the room, and repeated the same story over and over.

"So, you're from California?"

"Yes."

"And how old is your little boy?"

"Four."

"And the baby?"

"She's due in August."

"Ah, a little girl. So sweet. So, how do you like Shotgun Ridge?"

"I've not seen much of it, but Montana is very beautiful."

"That it is. And a better man you won't find than Wyatt Malone."

"That's nice to know."

"Sure was surprised to hear he'd advertised for a bride."

"Mmm."

Several times she'd caught herself before she'd said that Wyatt was surprised, too.

At first she hadn't known how to take the questioning, then realized it was simply their way. They were friendly and happy to welcome a newcomer into their fold. Thus, they'd want to exchange as much information as was humanly possible in the space of several minutes.

Her mind was spinning a bit, because, not only did Hannah give information, she'd received plenty of it, as well.

She'd learned that Henry Jenkins ran the feed store in town and Vernon and Vera Tillis owned the general store where folks bought their groceries and just about everything else a body could think of. Both Henry and Vern claimed to be older than dirt but were happy to report that they had all their teeth. Vera called them goats and advised Hannah to pay them no mind.

Ozzie Peyton was the mayor of Shotgun Ridge and owned a small but respectable ranch on the outskirts of town. He'd lost his wife Vanessa a few years ago and still keenly felt the loss.

They were all very glad Hannah and Ian had chosen Shotgun Ridge, and they were all very interested to know if she'd spoken with Iris Brewer yet, but oddly reluctant to expand on why they found that question so stirringly important.

Feeling as though she were about to enter a mine field, she finally made her way across the room to the kitchen where Iris was washing up the dishes.

"I understand you made the potato salad?"

Iris smiled, her pretty blue eyes filled with warmth. Nothing awful there. So, why was everyone so concerned about them meeting up?

"Yes. The egg gives it a different flavor. Plus I mix a few spices in with the mayonnaise. I'll write down the recipe if you're interested."

"Oh, I am. I'm Hannah Richmond."

"Yes, I know." Iris scrubbed at a stubborn spot on the pan, then stopped, her head lifting, her mouth curving into a smile of chagrin. "And I'm Iris Brewer. I forget that…well, everyone knows me. Lloyd and I run Brewer's Saloon in town."

"I've been there. Great cheeseburgers."

"Thank you." Iris wiped her hands on her apron, glanced through the opening that separated the kitchen from the church hall. "It's probably hard to tell so soon, but are you settling in all right? With Wyatt, I mean."

Hannah sighed and leaned against the counter. "I'm afraid there are some problems there."

Iris nodded.

"You know?"

"I know that Ozzie and his cronies got it in their heads to play matchmaker. I'm a little surprised that my Lloyd went along with it."

Hannah frowned. "Why?"

"Oh, you don't know, do you?"

"Know what?"

"Becky was our daughter. She was married to Wyatt."

Hannah felt hot and sick to her stomach. The clutch of guilt and embarrassment was quick and scalding.

"Oh, I'm sorry for your loss. And Wyatt doesn't want me." That came out wrong. But she didn't know her own thoughts at the moment. She felt like an intruder. Especially where this sweet woman was concerned.

"Now, dear, I'm not so certain that's true. I've watched him, and he looks at you with longing in his eyes."

"He doesn't even know me." Never mind the same was true for her and she felt a lot more than longing. She'd had several weeks of tracing his picture, of building dreams.

"Sometimes you don't have to know someone very long."

"This has got to be difficult…awkward for you. Because Wyatt's your son-in-law."

"I'll admit at first I had a twinge. But it's been four years."

"She must have been very special," Hannah said softly. "I can't imagine losing a child. If I lost Ian…" She took a breath, swallowed the immediate, uncontrollable lump that rose in her throat. "I don't think I could go on."

"Yes, you could. You do what you have to."

"I wouldn't want to."

"Your Ian is precious. I look at him and think this might be what Timmy would look like now. He would have been five this month."

Hannah reached out, took Iris's hands, yet didn't speak. There was nothing she could say. Nothing she knew *how* to say.

"I think you and your children will be good for Wyatt."

"I'm not so sure that's going to work out." She looked into Iris's eyes. "My husband wasn't a very good man. It's a long story, but the short of it is, I need to be loved. I can't and won't settle for less. At this point, I don't know if Wyatt's capable of giving me that."

"But you'll work on it."

"Yes. I do intend to." She said it softly, gently. She'd come here believing that love was possible—based on the letters she'd thought were from Wyatt. She wasn't ready to give up just yet. "Are you sure my being here doesn't bother you?"

"No, dear. Truly, it doesn't. And I'm probably just as surprised as you to realize that. Tell me about your family. Your mother."

"I lost my mother and father three years ago."

"Oh, I am sorry. You must miss them."

"Terribly. Every day I wonder if I'm making the right decisions, and I start to pick up the phone, then I remember. They say it gets easier. I haven't really found that to be true."

Iris wrapped her arms around Hannah and simply held her. The hug was genuine, touching, and it was all Hannah could do to keep from sobbing into this wonderful woman's shoulder. Baby hormones, she decided.

"I think the good Lord knew what he was doing when he put us in each other's path, Hannah Richmond."

"How's that?"

"I lost a daughter and grandson, and you lost a mother. Now here we are—the three of us. Perhaps we could stand in for one another to fill those gaping holes?''

This time Hannah's eyes did fill with tears. ''That's a beautiful thought, Iris. I'd like that very much.'' Oh, here was the acceptance and warmth she'd been seeking when she'd left her familiar life behind for the unknown.

Just then, she felt a lot more confident that she'd made the right decision in coming here.

HANNAH SAT on the front porch in a wooden swing suspended by chains, the creek of wood and metal as soothing as the peppermint tea steaming in her cup, teasing her senses. As it turned out, Vera Tillis was a gourmet tea lover and stocked the general store with quite a variety.

Wyatt had shown her around town a bit after church, but he'd been preoccupied, quiet and withdrawn.

His mood made her nervous.

She sipped her tea, inhaled the calming scent, her foot idly setting the porch swing in gentle motion. From here she could see the barn and the corral where Ian was frolicking like a puppy while Skeeter performed fancy rope tricks.

Satisfied that her son was safe and happy, she looked out over the horizon. The visual stimulation was everything she'd hoped for. She could just sit for days and stare off into the sunset—a sunset that wasn't shrouded in smog or hidden by houses and buildings and billboards.

The view went farther than the eye could see rather than slamming into a brick wall.

Here, there was peace.

Here, a soul could sing.

The call of a coyote carried on the wings of an evening breeze, raising the hairs on Hannah's arms. Odd how she could feel the slight punch of unease and the peaceful feel of rightness at the same time. The vastness should speak of loneliness, yet it spoke of home.

A cloud of dust drew her eye, and a horseman rode into the yard. Wyatt. Sitting tall in the saddle, his legs straddling the powerful animal, boots hooked in the stirrups, hat riding low over his forehead as though it were part of the man.

Her heart pumped harder at the sight of him.

Ian charged toward Wyatt and Hannah came up out of the porch swing, her heart now pounding with a mother's fear. My God, he was just a baby. That horse could step all over him, crush his tiny body... *Oh, stop it, Hannah.*

As she watched, Wyatt grinned and reached down just as Skeeter lifted Ian. Oh, he was going to give Ian a ride. She still felt nervous. And envious.

She wished she had the fearless nature of her son. Where had she learned to have such chicken tendencies? Was it the fear of being hurt? Emotionally as well as physically? Of losing?

She shook her head. She was no psychologist and shouldn't be trying to act like one.

Ian shrieked, his little face lit like the sun as Wyatt walked Tornado around the corral.

Please, God, she found herself praying. *Let it be right.*

With her arms wrapped around herself, she watched Wyatt Malone with her son. Even from this distance, she could hear Ian's little voice going non-stop and she smiled. Nobody could stay immune for long in Ian's presence. Her son was hard to resist, and it took mere minutes to fall in love with him.

From the way Wyatt was looking down at the boy and grinning, it appeared that he was halfway in love with the child already.

Now if only he'd look at her like that.

Difficult to do if he was going to ignore her. She'd have to make sure she made him notice her.

Pretty darn big goal seeing as how her stomach was stretched well beyond the snap of sexy jeans and un-suited to clingy silk.

She'd just have to make him notice other things—like what an asset she could be to his life, his ranch.

WYATT'S MUSCLES wept from the relentless beating they'd taken in the past two days. In an effort to keep his distance from Hannah, both emotionally and phys-ically, he'd pushed himself hard, garnering frowns from his ranch hands.

"Don't know what bee's in your shorts son, but when you push yourself like this, the men feel like they gotta work three times as hard."

Wyatt took off his hat and swiped the sleeve of his shirt over his forehead. He started to speak when a flash of pink caught his eye.

Arrested by the sight of her, he watched as Hannah

streaked across the yard toward the henhouse, skirting the shade of the cypress as though it were alive.

He shook his head, grinned despite himself.

"Most peculiar thing," Skeeter said. "She got something against shade? The boys are starting to think they got B.O. Sun goes behind the clouds and she backs up, regardless of who's standin' there talking to her."

Amusement licked at his insides. He had an idea why she did it, but he wasn't sure.

The startled, one-note feminine scream had him jamming his hat back on his head, his boots digging into the earth as he charged across the yard, Skeeter hot on his heels, Trevor and Steve coming from the opposite direction.

She ran out of the wooden coop, and he only had a split instant to note the waxen pallor of her skin before she literally climbed right up his body and into his arms.

With her legs wrapped around his hips this way, his body reacted like lightning, but he dismissed it.

"What is it?" He cradled her, tried to see if she was injured. He held her easily as she burrowed into him, her face in the crook of his neck, her warm breath puffing against his skin in shallow pants as though she'd run a marathon and couldn't quite catch her wind.

"Snake."

She said it softly. Tersely. And despite the fact that she had jumped into his arms and her chest was rising and falling against his—giving him way too many improper thoughts—her voice didn't tremble.

"A snake?"

"I *hate* snakes." This time revulsion quaked her body and her voice.

Wyatt stiffened, panic sweeping him like a freezing blizzard. "Did it get you?"

No answer.

"Sweetheart. Tell me. Look at me. Did it bite you?" He was trying to check now, but she wouldn't let go of her strangling hold on his neck.

She shook her head.

"'No' it didn't bite you, or 'no' you don't want me to look?"

"It didn't bite."

He let out the breath he hadn't realized he'd been holding. He'd dealt with rattlesnake bites before, but it wasn't pleasant. And to have it happen to a delicate woman—a *pregnant* woman—was unthinkable.

"I'm okay now," she said, loosening her arms.

His still held her firmly.

She unwrapped her legs from around his waist and he allowed her to slide down the front of his body, barely suppressing the groan that fought to escape. There was no way in hell she couldn't feel his arousal.

She looked up at him. Where before her face had been sheet-white, now her cheeks bloomed like a spring rose. And in her eyes was a need that matched his.

He looked away, noticing that Skeeter, Trevor and Steve were all watching with avid interest.

"Where's the snake?"

A slight shudder now. She pointed behind her. "In there. Big black thing. I'll have nightmares."

"Chicken snake." He glanced up and without having to be told, Trevor and Steve went into the hen-house to deal with it. Skeeter backed away to give them some privacy, which was a good thing, because if she moved from in front of him, everyone would see the painfully aroused state of his body.

"What the heck is a chicken snake?"

He put his arm around her, turned her and headed her away from the coop so that she wouldn't see what the men did with the snake. His mother had insisted he build the small structure so her hens would have proper facilities in order to sit or brood or produce, whatever their preference.

He thought again of how his mother would like Hannah. "It's a constrictor."

"Oh, Lord, those squeezing kind?"

"Yeah. They like rodents and lizards and eggs. A nuisance, but not poisonous."

"And babies."

"Excuse me?"

"They eat babies."

His brows shot up. "No, I don't think so."

"I read about it. These people had a pet boa and it got the baby. Another got the neighbor's little dog."

"Well, that sort of thing's never happened around here."

"That you know of," she muttered. "Do they get in there often?"

She looked so forlorn he wanted to hug her. "No. This time of year, coming out of hibernation, I imagine they're fairly hungry."

She sighed. "I thought gathering eggs would be a simple thing. Something I could excel at. Even King Tut is starting to give me a bit of room and respect. Which probably isn't saying much since he appears to be senile."

He knew he shouldn't laugh, and barely managed to contain the mirth. "He'd be insulted to hear you talk about him that way. He's a fairly young cock and considers himself pretty studly."

"Then we ought to get him a watch. His sense of timing is awful the way he crows at all hours of the night and morning."

He tucked his tongue in his cheek. "I'll ask him if he's interested."

Hannah elbowed him in the ribs. "Poke fun if you like. You're used to all this. I'm a novice." She grabbed his arm, pulled him in a short detour around a good-size rock propped against the fence. "I don't think the hairs on my arms are ever going to lay back down." She gave a delicate shudder. "If it wouldn't make me feel like such a ninny, I'd ask you to carry me."

"Be glad to oblige."

She bumped him with her shoulder again, charming him with her smile and her action. "I've embarrassed myself enough for one day, thanks."

"Are you saying you'd be embarrassed to have me carry you?" He had no idea why he was engaging in this conversation, encouraging it. He had no business.

Her withering look firmly slapped his ego back in place. Hell, he'd thought it would be considered macho and sexy to have her in his arms. Apparently, she wasn't thinking along those lines. And he shouldn't be, either.

"I'm supposed to be learning about ranching and such. Name one rancher's wife you know who has to be carted around the yard because she's afraid the snakes are lurking in the shade, determined to torment her."

He laughed at the drama of her voice and ignored the little zing that shot through him at her mention of being a rancher's wife.

"I might have spooked you unnecessarily. They're not lurking in the shade, so you don't have to avoid it. Just be aware and cautious, that's all. The snakes would just as soon not see you. Make a bit of noise and they'll stay out of your way."

"Oh, no. Don't give me that 'they're more scared of you than you are of them' speech. I had a friend who went to Florida and was *chased* by a water moccasin. *Chased,*" she stressed again.

"Well, you're safe here. No water moccasins on the ranch."

"What, you don't have water?"

"We've got water. In fact, there's a nice little creek not far that's great for picnics." Now why would he think of picnics? That was a family activity. And she wasn't going to be his family.

He was supposed to be concentrating on finding her another family. Another husband. He was supposed to be teaching her about ranching and the animals.

"Anyway, the guys are starting to think their hygiene's poor because you won't stand next to them."

"Oh, no. I didn't mean to offend."

"I imagine you'd have a hard time offending, Hannah. Half the men on this ranch are lovesick over you."

She looked at him sharply, the hope in her eyes nearly shouting the question: *But not you?*

He felt his heart squeeze, was reminded of his part in messing with her life. He couldn't bear to be the one to shatter her dreams. So he needed to keep his mind on his purpose.

And in the meantime, make sure he didn't shatter his own heart in the process.

"Where's Ian?"

"On the porch playing with the puppies." She nodded toward the house where Ian's dark head was bent over the bundle of fur balls frolicking around him, climbing over his lap like he was an obstacle course. His high-pitched giggle floated on the morning breeze, inviting company, a sound that would soften even the hardest of hearts.

Wyatt looked around and spotted Skeeter leaning against the corral fence, a piece of straw sticking out of his whiskered mouth. Steve and Trevor had already dealt with the snake and were back in the horse arena with Brant, who was putting a new cow pony through his paces.

"Hey, Skeeter."

"Yeah, boss." The old man walked over, his friendly gaze on Hannah. "Feeling better, missy?"

"Yes, thanks. Sorry I scared you all."

"No need to apologize. Them big old constrictors make my skin crawl, too. I'd a squawked like a chicken myself if I'd come face-to-face with the varmint.''

"I doubt that, but thank you for saying so, Skeeter.''

He held up a weathered hand. "Honest.''

"You busy right now?'' Wyatt asked. If Skeeter got any more sweet, he'd drip syrup from his weatherbeaten pores.

"Depends on what you want done.'' Skeeter grinned. The old man was as much the boss around here as Wyatt.

"I thought I'd introduce Hannah to Daisy, but Ian's about to hug those puppies to death. Mind keeping an eye on him while we're over at the barn?''

"Mind? Why, that boy's a pure pleasure. Talks more than's necessary,'' he teased, grinning at Hannah. "But I'd be mighty glad to watch after him for a bit. Give me a chance to take a load off these old feet.''

"Thanks, Skeeter.'' Wyatt steered Hannah toward the barn.

She looked back over her shoulder. "Are his feet all right?'' Worry colored her voice.

"Yeah. He'll complain up a storm, but that's just his way. He's got more stamina than Fancy—and just as much spit and vinegar.''

"Fancy—oh, the llama.'' Hannah flicked her hair behind her ear wishing she'd thought to grab a hair band. Although the sun cast a warm buttery glow over the land, the wind had some whip to it.

As they moved into the cooler interior of the barn, she inhaled the scent of horses and leather and hay. Tornado bobbed his head over the stall door and Wyatt spoke softly to the animal before moving on and stopping by an enclosure farther down.

Daisy turned out to be a pretty little chestnut mare with velvety eyes.

"I figured you can't ride since you're pregnant and all, but you can get used to the horses. Daisy's a sweetheart. You can groom her and get comfortable around her."

"She's beautiful." She hated the apprehension that welled up and was determined to be courageous— even if she had to pretend. "Can I pet her?"

"Sure. She'll love you for it. She'll stand here all day and let you rub on her."

"Smart girl. I'd love for someone to rub on me, too." She said the words without thought for how they would sound. And though her intention was to get this sexy cowboy to notice her, to fall for her, the suggestion made her blush.

She peeked at him, at his stillness, and laughed. "Relax. I'm not going to strip down right here."

"You could if you wanted." His voice was like gravel, soft and rough.

An arc of pure erotic sensation flared between them, holding her still, her gaze locked to his, her breath held, her hands trembling where they were poised to stroke the horse.

Daisy nudged Wyatt's shoulder and the movement jolted Hannah, breaking the spell.

Well, that was interesting, she thought. Progress. This was the second time today he'd gotten turned on. By her.

Lust, she decided, was a very nice stepping stone to love.

Chapter Seven

Wyatt made a Herculean effort to get his libido under control and his mind back on the lesson. He had an entirely different lesson in mind, though.

He couldn't remember the last time he'd wanted to kiss a woman so badly. He ached with it, used every ounce of his control to keep his hand on Daisy's smooth coat and not on Hannah's soft skin or plump breasts.

He cleared his throat, opened the stall door and carefully urged Hannah inside with him, giving her plenty of time to adjust at her own pace.

Apprehension and determination. Both flitted across her features. Man, he liked this woman's spirit. So honest. Nothing hidden.

"Go ahead and put your hands on her."

Tentatively, fingers trembling just a bit, she reached out and stroked Daisy's neck. "Oh!"

He smiled at the awe in her voice. "That's it. Talk to her if you like."

"She's so soft."

"Mmm." He put his hand over hers, urged her

palm to the blaze between Daisy's eyes, caught for a minute by the contrast of their hands. Hers smooth and white and soft, his rough and tanned and twice the size.

Daisy nodded and Hannah jerked, backing into him, her behind nestling right into his groin.

He ought to get an award for swallowing his groan, for not wrapping his arms around her waist and pulling her to him even tighter.

"Easy. She's not going to buck or kick or bite you or run you down."

Hannah smiled, moved away. "Let me guess. The females as well as the males on this ranch have manners."

"Yeah."

"So she'll just stand here nicely?"

"Sure. Now if you jump out at her and say 'boo' you'll scare her and she'll take off. She can get scared just like you and me. So don't be making sudden moves and you'll get along just fine. If you want to walk behind her, just put your hand on her and let her know you're there."

"Look at those big brown eyes," Hannah cooed. Her hand moved with more sureness now. "And soft lips. Warm. Cuddly." She inched closer still, hugged Daisy's neck, laid her cheek against the sleek surface.

Wyatt inhaled. The restriction in his jeans wasn't about to abate anytime soon. Her voice and her touch—though directed toward the horse—was running an erotic film in his mind.

In Technicolor.

With him and Hannah as the stars.

She turned, catching him off guard, her smile rivaling the sun. "Thank you for taking this time with me, Wyatt. I know you're busy."

He shrugged. "I don't mind."

And that worried him. Big time.

WYATT LOOKED UP from tagging the heifer's ear to see Hannah hanging sheets on a clothesline. He frowned, handed his tool to Trevor and started toward her.

Skeeter paused, watched a minute, then grinned. Wyatt kept walking.

She'd strung a cord from the satellite dish to the cottonwood tree. The wind whipped the sheets up and around the cord faster than she could get them pinned.

He snagged an end of the fabric, repositioned a pin.

She smiled. "Thank you."

"What are you doing?"

"Hanging out the sheets." Her expression indicated he was a bit slow—especially since he was standing there helping her accomplish the task.

"We have a dryer."

"Oh, I know that. But the smell of sunshine-fresh sheets from the clothesline is heavenly."

He raised a brow. "You hang out the wash at your place in California?"

"Are you kidding?"

"So why go to the extra trouble here?"

She shrugged, looking at him with uncertainty now. He felt like he'd been mean. "I thought it would be a nice touch. I guess it's more of a luxury for me, rather than a perk for you."

"No." The wind snatched the sheet out of his hand again and it nearly brushed the dirt. The cord was sagging. "I like the smell of sheets fresh from the line." Heck, he'd never even smelled them before. "Hang on a sec and I'll tighten this cord before you end up with it all on the ground and have to rewash it."

"Oh, I'm taking you away from your work again." She inspected the sagging cord as though daring it to fail her, her gaze measuring the distance between the bottom of the sheets and the patchy ground.

"No problem." He looped a stick through the slack rope and gave several twists, pulling the cord taut, securing it with a piece of twine.

"Still, I think…Billy, don't you dare!"

Startled, Wyatt whirled and lost his hold on the twine. The line sagged, aided by the goat who now had his mouth around a corner of the end sheet and was intent on a snack.

He grinned when she charged after the billy goat. She hummed a little sound of distress, but moved forward anyway, attempting to separate cotton from the goat's mouth.

"Bad, bad goat. Drop that sheet. I mean it!"

Wyatt was biting his lip now, but his shoulders were starting to shake. Man, she was cute. Still a little scared of that goat, but toughing it out anyway.

He moved forward to give her a hand.

"Stay where you are." She said. "I'll handle this."

"Yes, ma'am."

She whipped around to look at him, her brows

creasing. "Don't call me ma'am, and don't you dare laugh at me."

He swallowed. "Wouldn't dream of it."

She held out her hand to the goat as though she expected it to trot right over and drop the piece of sheet in her open palm. Evidently that's exactly what she intended.

"This is unacceptable behavior, Billy. We've spoken about manners just this morning, and already you've forgotten. You should be ashamed. Now stop that."

Amazingly enough, the goat dropped the sheet. Looking chagrined and apologetic, he sidled right over to her and butted her knee lovingly.

"Well, I'll be damned."

"Language, Wyatt."

His brows shot up. "It's a goat!"

"Yes, but a mannerless one. We're trying to teach here. He'll misunderstand."

His lip was nearly bleeding. "Were you a teacher?"

"No, but you don't need credentials to teach behavior."

"Of course not."

She patted the goat's head, and shifted back when it bumped her again. The more she shifted, though, the more the goat bumped her.

She sighed. "Okay, okay. That's enough for now. Go play or something." She did a little sidestep dance, but the goat took it as a game. The sidestep soon became a full dodge and a cute, softly pitched shriek escaped her lips.

She grabbed Wyatt's forearm, circled him, the goat mirroring her movements.

"This isn't working." There was a tremble in her tone, a combination of laughter and nerves. As she had after the snake incident, she nearly climbed up him, this time, though, stopping short and just pressing herself against him as though trying to become one.

His amusement rocketed straight into desire.

The goat stopped and looked at them in confusion at the halt of the game.

Hannah's forehead rested against his collarbone, her shoulders lifting and falling in a slow deep rhythm.

"Hannah?"

"Just give me a minute."

He didn't know if he could survive for a minute. Her pregnant stomach nestled against his belt. He could simply cup her bottom, lift just a bit, tilt, and she'd be pressed right to the heat of him. The hard heat of him.

As though they hadn't just been plastered together like flypaper and *one* of them wasn't so aroused he hurt, she stepped back, took a cleansing breath, turned and glared sternly at the goat.

"I am not playing. I'm bigger than you, and I have work to do. Go lay down!"

The goat stared.

"Don't look at me with those eyes. Ian tries it all the time and it doesn't work." She pointed. "Go."

And it went.

Hannah nodded and turned around, feeling terribly

proud of herself. Her gaze slammed right into Wyatt's.

His hazel eyes sizzled.

She went utterly still, though her gaze bobbed to belt level then back. *Oh. Oh, my.*

Mesmerized, she stood there with the sheets flapping around them like a stark white privacy screen and watched as Wyatt's arm extended, his hand cupping her cheek, his fingers wrapping around the back of her neck, drawing her closer with a hint of pressure.

She didn't need much urging. Ever since their kiss in the hallway, she'd ached to repeat it.

Time seemed to stand still. The smell of laundry detergent from the damp sheets swirled on the breeze, mingling with the pungent scent of animals and earth...and man.

His gaze was intense, unreadable. He was thinking this to death, she could tell. He wanted her, but he didn't want to. That, too, she could tell by looking at him, and the knowledge gave her power. She parted her lips, saw his eyes flare.

"What would it hurt?" she whispered.

The shake of his head was barely there. "More than you know."

Closer now, his breath becoming her breath. "We could...take a chance."

"I'm not a man who takes chances often."

She licked her lips, moved ever so slightly closer, her blood pumping so hard it made her dizzy. If she didn't feel him, taste him, she'd die. "Just for a minute, then."

"Just for a minute," he repeated, a mere breath, as his lips closed over hers.

Oh, the taste of him was heaven. His mouth moved over hers, his tongue tracing the seam of her lips. His chest rose and fell in rhythm with hers, yet he worshipped her mouth in slow, easy strokes as though they had all day, all year, to just stand there and nibble.

His kiss sent a thrilling ripple from her head to her toes. It was the most erotic thing she'd ever engaged in. She had no idea a kiss, just a simple meeting of mouths, could arouse so. She ached with it.

Going on tiptoe, she wound her arms around his neck, angled her head, dove into paradise without a thought for her surroundings or possible audience. There could have been a blizzard around them and she'd have never known.

His palms traveled from the underneath side of her raised arms, down to her rib cage, his fingers flexing against her back, his thumbs barely brushing the outer swell of her breasts.

On a moan of pure masculine sensory pleasure, he drew her even closer, wrapped her in his strong embrace, set her on fire and cherished her at the same time.

This is what a kiss should be, she thought dimly.

The ground shook beneath her feet. Earthquake, she thought, nearly smiling against his mouth. But she couldn't smile. She could only whimper, pressing closer, angling this way and that, holding on to a piece of heaven while the ground shook and trembled beneath her.

A shout and a whistle rent the air.

Wyatt jerked and reared back, yet her arms were still wound around him, holding him to her chest, her plump breasts pillowed against him.

Something penetrated his consciousness, but for the life of him, he couldn't get his brain to focus. He could have sworn the earth moved.

"What's that?" she whispered.

His mind was blank. He nearly took her lips again.

"Are we having an earthquake?"

"Earth—?" He looked around, his brain connecting with reality. Finally.

A rumble of hooves, nervous mooing, calves calling to their moms as riders on horseback urged them along, herding them into a pen.

"Not an earthquake." Even to his own ears, his voice sounded thick and slurred, as though the words were whispered from a distance. "Uh, we're doing some early branding today—some of the babies that were born in the calving shed."

"Oh."

Sun reflected off saddles, and bridles glinted like mirrors. Red dust, stirred by hundreds of hooves, swirled in the air, coating Hannah's freshly washed sheets.

He saw the moment she noticed, saw the distress that clouded her features.

"That's why we use the dryer."

The flash of defeat that flickered over her features gave him a punch.

"Hey. You didn't know."

"It seems that there's not much that I *do* know."

He pressed his fingertips to her chin, tipped it gently up. "That's why you're here, remember? To learn. And you got that crazy goat to mind. That's something."

A flash of pride replaced the defeat. She took a breath, the action raising her impressive chest.

Wyatt nearly lost his train of thought again.

"You better get back to work. I didn't mean to interrupt."

"You didn't."

She gave him a pitying look.

"Well, you didn't. I'm the one who came over here. You were doing fine without me."

She thought about that for a moment, looked at her crudely constructed clothesline. "You're right. I'd have noticed it sagging and figured out a way to fix it."

"Of course you would."

She nodded, feeling better. "Maybe next time you can tell me when you're planning to make the cattle run around like that. I'll schedule laundering the sheets for another day."

He didn't have the heart to tell her these dusty dirty conditions were pretty much a constant—unless it was raining or snowing. And in those instances she wouldn't be hanging out the sheets anyway.

At least not on his ranch.

He bent down and picked up his hat from the ground where it had fallen when she'd wound her arms around him in that mind-numbing kiss.

Man alive, he was in trouble.

HANNAH REWASHED the sheets and used the dryer this time. The floors were clean and the countertops shining. Behind the house, the flower beds were blooming with tulips and lilies. Wyatt's mother must have planted bulbs last fall and now that the ground had thawed, the yard was bursting with color.

Finding a vase, she cut some of the colorful blooms and assembled an arrangement for the kitchen table and the end table in the living room. Happy with the results, she decided the men could benefit from a little springtime in the bunkhouse.

Ian came tiptoeing through the kitchen, a puppy in each arm. She smothered a laugh. He obviously thought he was invisible or something.

"Where are you going with those puppies, young man?"

"Huh?" He looked up at her, all innocence.

She pointed to the animals in his arms lest he think she'd suddenly gone blind.

"They was cold."

"They need their mommy."

"Yep. Skeeter said so, too. So, Lady's gonna come and live in my room."

"I don't know, son. Wyatt might not want the dogs in the house."

"Uh-huh. They like it in here."

"I'm sure they do, but—"

"I-it's okay, Mom. Skeeter said."

He was so darn cute, how could she resist or deny him? As if to add her approval, Lady pawed open the back door that Ian had left ajar and trotted in, panting happily, looking at Ian and Hannah as though expecting praise for giving birth to such fine-looking offspring.

Hannah smiled. "Okay. You all go get settled. But we'll have to clear this with Wyatt later on. And if he says they have to sleep in the barn, we have to mind. Understand?"

"'Kay." He addressed the puppy under his left arm. "'Kay, sweetie? You get to sleep wif me and S'nook and everybody, cuz Wyatt says."

Hannah started to remind that Wyatt hadn't "said" yet, but held her peace. At least he wasn't asking to have the goat in the house.

"I'm going out to the bunkhouse. Do you know where that is?"

"Yep. Skeeter showed me. And Twevor and me played wif the checkers."

"All right. I won't be long, but if you need me, come get me."

She'd have to find out if they needed a box or newspapers or something for the pups. She didn't know the first thing about housebreaking puppies. Maybe she ought to check with Skeeter on that.

She'd interrupted Wyatt enough for one day.

Gathering some cleaning supplies, she went out the back door, clipped some more flowers and headed toward the bunkhouse. She'd been in there earlier and it was a disaster area. Rather than a pail and water, she'd be better off with a shovel.

FILTHY AFTER spending the afternoon cleaning, Hannah showered and changed before heading back downstairs to put the final touches on dinner. She was going to have a hard time prying Ian away from Lady and her pups.

She'd just spritzed on perfume when her hands froze and her heart kicked up a notch.

Someone was calling for help.

Not Ian. Not a masculine voice.

It came again. She charged out of the room, adrenaline urging her on, making her light-headed.

She gave a squeal of fright when Wyatt came around the corner, his hands shooting out to steady her.

"We've got to stop meeting this way," he teased, grinning, then sobered when he noticed her distress. "What is it?"

"Someone's calling for help. A woman it sounds like." The cry came again. "Hear that?"

Head cocked, hat tipped back, he listened, then smiled. "That's the peacock."

"The peacock?"

"The peacock," he confirmed, his grin stretching.

Hannah felt like an idiot. An extremely common occurrence lately. Her brows rose as she attempted to cover her naiveté. "Is he in need of help?"

He shook his head slowly.

"He just likes to give the new woman on the block a heart attack?"

His gaze dropped to her mouth. "Evidently."

Hannah's heart nearly leaped out of her chest. Would they have an instant repeat of the other day—right here in the upstairs hallway?

Unsure, she took a half step back, her shoulders coming up against the wall. There was something

PLAY
RUN FOR THE ROSES

...and you can get

FREE BOOKS and a FREE GIFT!

Turn the page and let the race begin!

PLAY
RUN
FOR THE
ROSES

and get
THREE FREE GIFTS!
HOW TO PLAY:

1. With a coin, carefully scratch off the silver box at the right. Then check the claim chart to see what we have for you — **2 FREE BOOKS** and a **FREE GIFT**—**ALL YOURS FREE!**

2. Send back the card and you'll receive two brand-new Harlequin American Romance® novels. These books have a cover price of $4.25 each in the U.S. and $4.99 each in Canada, but they are yours to keep absolutely free.

3. There's no catch. You're under no obligation to buy anything. We charge nothing — ZERO — for your first shipment. And you don't have to make any minimum number of purchases — not even one!

4. The fact is, thousands of readers enjoy receiving books by mail from the Harlequin Reader Service®. They enjoy the convenience of home delivery...they like getting the best new novels at discount prices, BEFORE they're available in stores... and they love their *Heart to Heart* subscriber newsletter featuring author news, horoscopes, recipes, book reviews and much more!

5. We hope that after receiving your free books you'll want to remain a subscriber. But the choice is yours — to continue or cancel, any time at all! So why not take us up on our invitation, with no risk of any kind. You'll be glad you did!

Visit us online at
www.eHarlequin.com

This surprise mystery gift
Could be yours **FREE** –
When you play
RUN for the ROSES

Scratch
Here
See Claim Chart

YES! I have scratched off the silver box. Please send me the 2 FREE books and gift for which I qualify! I understand that I am under no obligation to purchase any books, as explained on the back and opposite page.

RUN for the ROSES	Claim Chart
👑 👑 👑	2 FREE BOOKS AND A MYSTERY GIFT!
👑 👑	1 FREE BOOK!
👑	TRY AGAIN!

NAME (PLEASE PRINT CLEARLY)

ADDRESS

APT.# CITY

STATE/PROV. ZIP/POSTAL CODE

354 HDL C25P

154 HDL C25F
(H-AR-OS-06/00)

DETACH AND MAIL CARD TODAY!

The Harlequin Reader Service® — Here's how it works:

Accepting your 2 free books and gift places you under no obligation to buy anything. You may keep the books and gift and return the shipping statement marked "cancel." If you do not cancel, about a month later we'll send you 4 additional novels and bill you just $3.57 each in the U.S., or $3.96 each in Canada, plus 25¢ delivery per book and applicable taxes if any.*
That's the complete price and — compared to cover prices of $4.25 each in the U.S. and $4.99 each in Canada — it's quite a bargain! You may cancel at any time, but if you choose to continue, every month we'll send you 4 more books, which you may either purchase at the discount price or return to us and cancel your subscription.

*Terms and prices subject to change without notice. Sales tax applicable in N.Y. Canadian residents will be charged applicable provincial taxes and GST.

If offer card is missing write to: Harlequin Reader Service, 3010 Walden Ave., P.O. Box 1867, Buffalo NY 14240-1867

BUSINESS REPLY MAIL
FIRST-CLASS MAIL   PERMIT NO. 717   BUFFALO, NY

POSTAGE WILL BE PAID BY ADDRESSEE

HARLEQUIN READER SERVICE
3010 WALDEN AVE
PO BOX 1867
BUFFALO NY 14240-9952

NO POSTAGE
NECESSARY
IF MAILED
IN THE
UNITED STATES

very sensual—erotic even—about meeting in the hall-way, her back to the wall, an incredibly sexy cowboy boxing her in.

She licked her lips, saw his eyes flare, saw the restraint there, too.

The man held himself on a tight rein.

"This isn't a good idea," he said softly, even though he moved closer, rested a palm against the wall right beside her head, leaned in.

The thrill that shot through her heated her blood and brought a blush to her cheeks and neck. She wanted to be sophisticated. The blush of inexperience—or perhaps shyness—annoyed her.

"I hear you've been working in the bunkhouse."

His voice was soft and sexy, his breath brushing her lips. Just two inches and his mouth would be on hers.

Her palms flattened against the wall behind her. Had he asked a question? The bunkhouse. "Yes."

His brows lifted, inviting elaboration.

"I thought the guys would appreciate having the place spruced up a bit."

"You shouldn't be working so hard."

"I don't mind. I'm enjoying it." She took a deep breath, watched his eyes slowly track the rise and fall of her breasts. "Were the flowers too feminine a touch?"

It seemed to take an eon before his gaze made the incredibly arousing journey back to her eyes. Dear heaven, this man was going to reduce her to liquid without even touching her. That was potent stuff.

"They're raving about the flowers," he said quietly. "I think they're all a little in love with you."

But she wanted Wyatt to fall in love with her. "You're not thinking about matchmaking with your ranch hands, are you?"

He shook his head. "I don't think you'd be happy in the bunkhouse."

She didn't bother to point out that she and whoever could move. He didn't need any new ideas introduced into his head.

He was obviously still determined to give her away. And she was just as determined to get him to keep her.

"For a man who truly loved me, I'd live with him in a tent," she said softly.

She gave her words a moment to sink in, to plant a seed, then ducked under his arm, hiding a smile when he frowned.

She'd give a lot for another one of those toe-curling kisses, but no sense in being totally easy to get.

Strategy, she thought as she headed toward the stairs, leaving him gazing after her like a man with a powerful hunger. "Dinner's in half an hour."

Chapter Eight

Wyatt decided he was going to get fat on Hannah's cooking. She had a tendency to use elaborate sauces to mix strange flavors and textures. Combinations that sounded awful.

But sounding and tasting were two different things. The crisp green beans with garlic and slivered almonds were a perfect compliment to the tender chicken breasts baked in tarragon and some kind of fruity sauce. Warm bread, cheesy potatoes and plenty of everything on the table made it a hearty meal. A sophisticated meal.

"Is it okay?"

"It's great. Makes me feel like I'm eating at a fancy restaurant instead of in the kitchen of my cattle ranch."

The timer on the oven sounded and she grabbed a hot pad, removing a pie that had his mouth watering.

"By the time we're finished with dinner, it should be cool enough to eat."

The fear for his waistline grew.

"Pretty good eats, don't you think, partner?" he

asked Ian. The boy was being awfully quiet, which was suspicious. He kept peeking up as though he were hiding something under the table.

"Yep."

"Ian, don't you have something to ask?" Hannah coached, sitting back down at the table.

Ian shook his head.

Wyatt hid a grin, ducked his head and looked under the table.

Ian's fork paused. He too, ducked and looked, meeting Wyatt's gaze under the tablecloth. Chinook, who was laying at their feet—thrilled with Ian in residence—perked his ears, giving a canine grin of anticipation that they might be about to embark on some new and fun game.

Wyatt winked and Ian toppled out of his chair giggling.

"Oh," Hannah groaned, her hand shooting out to catch her son. "Settle down, Ian."

"Leave him be," Wyatt said. "That was my fault."

"I got the puppies in my room to s-sleep wif me. Did you know th-that I got a cut?" He held his finger up for inspection, and Wyatt tried not to laugh at the sly change of subject.

He'd noticed that Lady and her pups were missing from the barn, but Skeeter had already told him the boy had spirited the animals into the house.

Now, evidently Ian thought he could impart the information and at the same time run interference and distract.

Wyatt cupped the single digit Ian practically

shoved up his nose, and inspected the minute cut with the solemn gravity of a funeral parlor director. Chinook sat patiently and gave a little whine as though to add his compassion. Sitting, the dog was nearly the height of Ian.

"This here's serious business. Suppose we need to run you into town and get Doc Hammond to give it a stitch?"

Ian's eyes widened. He considered, discarded. "It's just a w-wittle baby cut."

"Are you sure? Maybe you need a tetanus shot or something."

Ian sucked in a gasp, ducked under the table, and popped up in Hannah's lap. Chinook's tags jingled as he raced to keep up, paws skidding on the tile floor before he sat politely by Hannah's side.

"Kiss it," Ian demanded, nearly poking her mouth with his finger. She obliged.

"All better," he said, looking across the table at Wyatt as though daring him to dispute. "Can da puppies s-stay i-i-in—"

"Slow down, sweetie," Hannah advised gently, pecking a kiss to the top of his hair.

"They like it in my room. And I won't give him no more raisins."

"You gave the puppy raisins?" Hannah asked.

"Yep." Ian's eyes sparkled, his tiny little teeth gleaming as he grinned. "And he pooped."

"Oh, honey. You mustn't feed the puppies food from the pantry—or the refrigerator," she added, knowing what a sharp mind he had.

"But he wanted a snack."

"For the first little while, puppies snack on their mother's milk," Wyatt said.

Ian slipped out of Hannah's lap and skipped around to stand by Wyatt as though this were a better vantage point to hear from, as though the sound of the words wouldn't travel the width of the table.

"Could they have some cookies wif their milk?"

Wyatt shook his head and ran his hand over Ian's silky cap of hair, feeling his own insides go soft.

There was something about this boy that drew him, despite his intentions otherwise. Ian had the same coloring and dark hair that Timmy had. Was that the draw? Is this what his son would have looked like?

Feeling like a swarm of vicious bees had attacked his chest, Wyatt deliberately blanked those thoughts. It wasn't wise to get attached. To love someone fiercely and to lose them was a pain too hard to bear.

"No cookies. Their tummies aren't ready to eat anything yet. They just want to drink. Tell you what. After dinner we'll go up and make sure their beds are fixed right, and I'll tell you all I know about puppies and what they should do—or not do—on the floor of the bedroom."

Ian went into a gale of giggles, a sound that never failed to bathe Wyatt in cheer. Coming on the heels of his melancholy, it was a balm to his crushed soul. If a person could bottle this gaiety, there'd be no need for antidepressant drugs. Just open the top, let out the innocent, unrestrained mirth, and be infused with good humor for the rest of the week.

"I gotta go tell 'em not to poop and barf on the floor."

Ian started to charge out of the room. Hannah's voice stopped him on a skid.

"What about dinner?"

"I eated the green ones. Pwease, Mommy?" His tone turned grave—if such a thing was possible for a small boy's underdeveloped vocal cords. "I gotta tell that puppy no more poopin' in the house," he repeated.

Hannah sighed. "And no more raisins."

"'Kay."

"All right. You may go."

He gave a shout of joy. "C'mon, S'nook!" Dog and boy raced from the room.

Wyatt shook his head. "He doesn't believe in walking."

"No, I think he's of the mind that he needs to pack as much as humanly possible into each minute. And in order to do that he has to run."

"And talk."

"And talk," she agreed, smiling. "Is he getting on your nerves?"

"No. Just the opposite. He amazes me, though. All that running and talking—the perpetual motion—wears him out. I had him up on the horse and one minute he was leaning against my chest, his mouth going like a motor, and midsentence he quit talking and nearly slumped off the horse. Don't laugh."

She did anyway. "He does that all the time."

"Well, he nearly gave me a heart attack. I panicked and grabbed him, and he came wide-awake, his eyes blinking like a barn owl's. Then quick as you please, as though he hadn't just dozed off, he started chattering again. Shook me up some, but it was the cutest thing I've ever seen."

"Yeah. He's pretty cute." Motherly pride filled her voice.

"You've done a good job with him, Hannah."

"Thank you." She stood to clear their dishes and switch on the coffeepot. "Sit," she ordered when he started to get up.

"I can help with the dishes."

"Dessert before dishes. It's a rule." She brought the blackberry pie to the table and set it on a hot pad. "I found some frozen berries in the freezer. You've got quite a selection out there."

The chest freezer was another part of Wyatt's ranch that tapped into her cozy memories. Aunt Shirley's chest freezer had been out in the detached garage, the cool interior of the structure musty smelling, the ice two inches thick around the walls of the chest. And among the deer, beef, various other meats, fruits and vegetables, was a stash of Fudgsicle pops. Hannah and Tori had nearly fallen into the deep chest head-first digging for them.

Wyatt's freezer held similar contents—in great abundance. All except for the chocolate pops. And that, Hannah could probably remedy next time she went to town.

"I usually keep it stocked pretty well. Never know when you'll get caught in bad weather and not be able to get to town for a while."

"Makes sense. Plus, I've realized it's not all that convenient just to run to town if you've forgotten something."

He looked at her oddly for a minute. "I forget you're used to being in the city with markets and conveniences around each corner. Here, it's a way of life to travel a bit to get what you need. I never even think about it."

"Everyone's comfortable with the way they're raised." She slid thick wedges of steaming pie onto plates and retrieved the ice cream out of the kitchen freezer. "What I want to know, though, is how you keep this stuff from melting before you can get it home?"

"Ice chest." He watched her move efficiently around his kitchen, the homey sight at war with the image that kept popping in his head of the two of them up against the wall.

"Oh. Clever."

"If folks are comfortable with what they've been raised on, why aren't you?" Why was she intent on a life-style she knew so little about?

"I'm an oddity, I guess. Stress will make perfectly sane people wig out."

He raised his brows at the drama in her voice. "Were you wigging out?"

"Yes." She used her thumb to push the ice cream off the spoon onto the pie. "I hate to admit it, but each day I felt like I was coping less and less. It's hard to say exactly why or what was causing it."

"I'd imagine getting a divorce and being pregnant is enough to bring even the strongest women down a notch." Unable to help himself, he snagged her hand, brought it to his mouth. "You've got a drip of ice cream.'' He licked the sticky sweet cream from the pad of her thumb. "Right there."

She went absolutely still, her lips parted, her misty green eyes following every movement he made. He might have smiled at her stunned expression, but he was a little dazed himself.

The yip-yip of a coyote drifted through the window, breaking the spell.

She took a breath, pulled her hand away.

He reached for his fork, surprised how unsteady his own hand was, and nearly moaned as the homemade pie dazzled his taste buds.

"So, what did you do for work where you lived? Or did you have a job? I know you said your ex was an attorney."

She put away the ice-cream carton, poured coffee and sat back down before answering. "Yes, Allan was in a high-income bracket, but he never felt like we had enough. He liked to spend and entertain. So I worked at a shipping port doing clerical work for a company that paid me an obscenely huge wage."

"Obscenely huge, huh?" With his fork he pointed to where her ice cream was melting atop her pie.

"Well, it was much better than average. Great benefits." She spooned a bite of dessert, toyed with the puddles of white that smeared her plate, glancing covertly at her thumb and then at his mouth.

"And the problem?" he asked, trying not to be aroused by her thoughts. Because crazy as it seemed, he could *see* what she was thinking. About him licking her fingers. Wondering if he'd do it again if she were to dip them into her plate.

And he would. In a heartbeat. And that's not all he'd want to lick....

"It was tedious work," she said, jerking him back to attention. "No challenge. I was cooped up in a windowless office. Even going outside on break was boring, just a sea of asphalt parking lots, the smell of diesel from eighteen-wheelers lined at the gates waiting to drop off their containers to be loaded onto the ships, a freeway overpass mere yards away jammed night and day with too many cars."

Hearing her describe it, he realized she'd have been wilting like a flower in the Sahara. "So you opted for the Big Sky Country."

"It's beautiful here. Different. Peaceful. Definitely has atmosphere."

"You don't have to convince me. I can't imagine living anywhere else."

"You work very hard, though, and in terrible weather conditions sometimes."

He shrugged. "As you said, it's what a person's used to. I grew up here, never knew any other type of life. This one fulfills me, so much so that I'd never even consider something else."

"That's such a wonderful way to feel. Everyone should be in love with their life, their work."

"And you definitely weren't." He hesitated. "Uh, how are you fixed for money? I'm assuming Allan's paying you child support for Ian—" He stopped, his brows drawing together when she shook her head. "He's not?"

"No. After the divorce papers came, he called and told me not to expect child support payments. He gave me the house and my car and the money in our checking account. I sold the house to pay off the mortgage and the car to pay off the loan, then bought the SUV and came here to start over.''

''There are laws to make him pay. These are his kids.''

''He's somewhere in Jamaica—out of reach. And he doesn't want his kids.''

''That's inexcusable.''

''That's Allan.''

If Wyatt's brows got any lower, they'd cover his eyes. ''Doesn't sound to me like you came out on the best end of the stick.''

''Oh, but I did. I got Ian and my baby. So don't go feeling guilty again, Wyatt. Coming here was my choice.''

''Based on letters you thought I wrote.''

''True. But I have savings and stock market investments. The insurance from my last job will see me through the birth of this baby.'' She pressed a hand to her swollen stomach. ''So I'm not destitute. And I have skills to get work.'' Though she hadn't thought about working. Ozzie—masquerading as Wyatt—had told her the ranch would be her work. Being a wife and mother and companion would be her work.

In today's climate of feminism and two-income families, it wasn't always politically correct or even feasible to want to be a homemaker. But that's exactly what Hannah wanted.

A loving career as a mother and a rancher's wife.

By coming to Montana, she'd taken a big chance

with her life and that of her kids. Gambled on a dream. On a man. Her cowboy.

But the rules of the game had changed and now, basically, she was here at Wyatt's ranch exchanging cooking and cleaning for room and board.

And instruction on ranch life.

He was training her to be someone else's wife.

And she desperately wanted to be his.

"OHMYGOSH, ohmygosh, ohmygosh!" Hannah quickly shut the door that blocked the kitchen from the rest of the house, and sprinted out the front door. Ian was on the porch.

"Stay right here, Ian. Don't go in the house." She continued down the porch steps and ran across the yard, dodging puddles left by the small rainstorm that had passed through overnight.

As though he could sense her coming, Wyatt looked up from the horse he was about to mount, saw her and was now striding just as quickly in her direction, meeting her halfway.

"Slow down, Hannah. You could fall. Running can't be good for the baby." His hands wrapped around her shoulders to steady, to soothe. The brim of his hat shaded his eyes, but couldn't disguise his concern.

"I'm fine." She wished she had a moment, or the sanity, to bask in his genuine protectiveness. But her mind could only concentrate on one thing.

A furry, horrible thing.

"You're not fine. What's wrong?"

"Skunk..." Her hands were shaking and so was

her voice. Her lungs wouldn't seem to fill with enough air, yet she labored as though she'd just run a mile.

Lord have mercy, this was not in her fantasy brochure.

"What?"

She swallowed, tried to steady her voice, made every effort to speak slowly and rationally, without fear or revulsion.

"There's a skunk in the kitchen. I apologize for continually interrupting your work, but—but would you please go shoo it out?"

Wyatt felt his lips twitch. "Darlin' you don't *shoo* a skunk."

"Okay, poor choice of words. And don't you dare laugh at me. Even I know what happens when you get too close to one of those creatures! However, that's the extent of my knowledge, and I'd like it out of my kitchen, please."

My kitchen. He couldn't quite define how her possessive choice of words made him feel.

"Best thing to do is leave the doors open and wait till he wanders back out—and hope he doesn't decide to cozy up in the rest of the house first."

"I shut the kitchen door, so he's hemmed in. I don't think the back door is wide-open, though. Ian must have left it ajar." She grabbed a strand of hair that blew in her face. "How long do you suppose the skunk will take to, uh, wander? I've got stuff to do."

"Hard to say. I'll go open the back door all the way."

He started across the yard and realized she was

following him. He smiled. Every day he was a little more charmed by this city woman who'd burst into his life uninvited—at least by him. He didn't want to feel these soft feelings, but they just wouldn't quit, no matter how many talks he had with himself.

He paused, turned, and she nearly slammed into his chest. His hand shot out to steady her. "You might want to stay clear. No telling how close he is to the back door."

"You mean he might spray you?"

"Could."

"Should you get someone else to help you?"

"No sense in two of us getting a stink bath."

"Oh. Of course not. I'm so sorry about this."

"It's not your fault, Hannah. Why don't you make sure Ian stays on the porch?"

She reversed directions, mounted the steps and watched from there, noting that Ian was preoccupied with the puppies and hadn't caught wind of what was going on. Thank goodness. He'd probably want to chase the darn skunk.

The billy goat wandered into the yard, chewing as usual. Heaven only knows what he was eating. That silly goat was always munching on something. It was a wonder he wasn't as big as a steer. And how he kept getting loose from his leash was a constant baffle. The darn animal was a highly skilled escape artist.

"Billy, no. Don't go over there. Come here. That's a good goat." Reluctant to leave the safety of the porch, she nevertheless went down the steps so Billy wouldn't come up. Next thing he'd be wanting to come in the living room and sit on the furniture. He was entirely too free on the grounds as it was. No sense allowing him to think he could have the run of the house, too. He'd probably eat the couch.

"Why don't you go over there and torment the rooster? He's entirely too full of himself. Chase him a bit and bring him down a peg or two, hmm?" She shoved, urging the goat away from the house and away from Wyatt's direction.

It seemed that each day she was bombarded with something new. And though she'd asked for this, idealized this life-style, it was a lot to assimilate in one short week.

First the introduction to the farm and ranch animals. Then it was snakes and peacocks. Now the skunk. Never mind the lovesick goat intent on eating everything in sight.

All these new experiences were exhilarating yet daunting, and invariably surrounding or attached to some kind of feathers, fur or scales.

She wondered what could be next, then realized she hadn't interacted with the llama yet. Peachy.

She was going to master these animals, come to friendly terms with them, or die trying.

Except for the snakes and skunks. She had to draw the line somewhere.

Wyatt came back around the house to the front porch, feeling his heart soften when Ian popped up from playing with the puppies.

"Hi, Wyatt!" he chirped, bouncing up and down, raising his arms. "You could pick me up!"

"I don't know. I might not have enough muscles."

Wyatt lifted the boy, perching him on a shoulder, and Ian giggled.

"Yeah! I'm way, way big up to the sky! I'm stwong, too." He plucked off Wyatt's hat and transferred it to his own head, his face nearly disappearing under the Stetson.

"Ian, calm down," Hannah admonished.

"'Kay. See my p-puppies, Wyatt? They're sleepin'. They got tired."

"Then you ought to let them have a nap." This little boy was so cute and Wyatt fought the intense feelings that welled in him. The sound of Ian's voice, his little-boy smell, his constant questions and hero worship, his mischievous streak, were all part of a package that Wyatt had once dreamed about.

But not anymore. Those dreams were dead and buried.

"Any luck with the skunk?" Hannah asked.

"The door's open. It's a waiting game right now." He noticed that Skeeter and the men were still in the corral waiting for him. But Hannah was trapped on the porch and he was about to go move part of the herd to a closer pasture. "How do you guys feel about hanging out with me for the day?"

"I've interrupted you enough."

"Hannah, I don't mind." He saw Skeeter start in their direction, and when Ian waved exuberantly and nearly wiggled them both off balance, he set the boy on his feet. Like a gamboling puppy, Ian skipped off the porch and met Skeeter, bouncing around the old cowboy's legs, asking questions and imparting information without pause, never waiting for answers or affirmations.

Skeeter grinned and stopped a few feet away from the porch. "You coming, boss?"

"Actually, I was just trying to talk Hannah into joining us. Got a curious skunk playing house in the kitchen."

"That'll never do." Skeeter's gaze bobbed to Hannah's stomach. "Don't know how advisable it'd be for Miss Hannah to ride, though."

"I could ride," Ian said.

Wyatt smiled, an idea taking form. The adventure would be perfect for the boy. "Hannah and I can take the truck."

"What are we talking about here?" Hannah asked.

"We're going to round up part of the herd, park 'em closer to home and ready them for branding."

"You want us to go on a cattle drive?"

"Just a short one. It'll only take part of the day."

"Not a bad idea," Skeeter said. "Ian, here, can ride out with me."

"On a horse?" Hannah asked faintly.

"Sure. He'll be safe as a kangaroo in its mama's pouch."

"Yeah!" Ian shouted.

"How safe is that?"

"A bit bouncy, but protected."

"Please, Mama?" Ian looked up at her with such hope she knew she'd have to set aside her own fears.

She trusted Skeeter. And she trusted Wyatt. If he didn't feel it was safe for Ian to ride, he'd say so.

She looked at Wyatt. "Are you sure?"

''Skeeter's main job is to ride herd on the boys. He'll only be traveling at a walk. It'll be an easy ride. You and I will take the truck. It'll do you good to get out of the house. See a little more of the countryside, more of the double M.''

''Should I change?''

He looked down at her tennis shoes and jeans, the lightweight sweater that skimmed her thighs. Everywhere his gaze touched was like a physical caress. ''You're fine like you are. What do you say?''

She glanced at Skeeter. ''Are you sure you don't mind taking Ian?''

''Don't mind a bit.''

She nodded, feeling excitement build. ''Okay. Ian, you mind Skeeter, now.''

'''Kay.'' His grin rivaled the sun as he hop-skipped alongside Skeeter toward the corral and the saddled horses.

Wyatt put a hand at Hannah's waist and guided her off the porch, then held open the door of the crewcab pickup. The men on horseback got a head start.

''We'll check the drops first and catch up,'' he told her, starting the truck.

''What on earth are the drops?'' She kept her eyes on her son who was mounted in front of Skeeter on a sleek-looking chestnut horse.

''Calves. We've separated the heifers that are still pregnant and parked them nearby in case there're problems. Several times a day, we check that group for new baby calves and any signs of mamas in distress that need to be moved to the calving shed.''

''Oh.'' The suspension on the truck was sturdy, and

though the ride was bumpy, it was smoother than being on horseback. Hannah felt a bit of anxiety when the men on horseback turned in the opposite direction.

"Relax. They'll be fine. And we'll meet up with them in a bit."

She smiled self-consciously. "Am I that transparent?"

"You're a mother."

It pleased her that he understood. With the window down, Hannah appreciated the sweet song of nature around them. The light storm that had blown in and out last night left the air clean and fragrant. Raindrops dripped off the pine boughs that had been planted close to the house to serve as a windbreak. A woodpecker searched for a meal high in a tree. As they rolled along the road by a creek, she feasted her eyes on a field of yellow daisies waving in the sun.

Spring seemed to have bloomed on the landscape overnight. Puffy clouds scuttled by like silent ghosts in a bright-blue sky, holding court over a sea of green grass. A meadowlark burst into song atop a fence post and the border collie, Bandit, raced ahead of the truck, darting off to chase a grasshopper or some other insect.

"Are there a lot of baby cows still to be born?"

"Some. Most of the late ones are already in the pen where we can watch them, but you never know if you've missed a few. The guys ride the range several times a day and check on them."

They were following a rutted trail bordered by a fence on one side and the creek on the other. Wyatt slowed the truck by a fence post that was listing as though it were a causality of a hit-and-run vehicle.

He put the truck in park. "Hang on a second. Let me see if I can straighten that post." He grabbed a hammer and a pair of gloves out of the back and went over to attend to the downed fence.

From the open window of the truck, she watched him work, his hat pulled low over his brow shading his face from the sun, his shoulders straining at the seams of his chambray shirt as he tugged and pounded at the barbed wire and steel post.

She was struck again by how capable this man was. He took care of what was his and did a darn fine job of it. His hands could wield wire cutters or maneuver a two-thousand-pound bull. They could cradle a puppy, ruffle a little boy's hair, or reverently cup a woman's pregnant belly.

Her heart gave a skip when she recalled his touch, the way he looked at her. It was unique and totally new to her.

From her experience with men in the city—and Allan in particular—they were so preoccupied and stressed, they'd glance at a woman but never give her their full attention. Their minds would wander to stock quotes, legal briefs, computers or whatever— perhaps even their latest mistress as no doubt Allan's had.

Here, though, it was so different. Maybe it was the slower pace. More than likely, it was the man. Because when Wyatt Malone looked at her, he really *looked* at her. With his whole being and undivided attention. She had an idea he knew where she was at all times—aware.

Protective, but not smothering. It was thrilling.

Even more thrilling was imagining how he would be as a lover. Would he bring that single-minded intent to the bedroom? She was certain he would. Based on his soul-stirring kisses, this man would be a dream.

He was certainly her dream.

Chapter Nine

Wyatt tossed his tools in the bed of the truck and started the engine. "It's little things like that fence there that keeps us on our toes. Weather and the animals take their toll and it's all we can do to keep up with the repairs."

"With so many acres, why do you need the fences?"

"We have to keep the herds sectioned off. And we don't want our cows straying onto the neighbors' land."

She laughed softly. "It's hard to picture that image, with your neighbors being so far away."

"Yeah, but Cherry's land borders mine. And she wouldn't appreciate my bulls surprising her heifers, especially the registered herd Wendell spent so many years building."

"That's the one you're after, right? The bull that can start you a herd like that?"

"Yeah. I'd give my eyeteeth to own Casanova. There are other registered studs out there, but there's something about Casanova that draws me. He's different. And the stock he produces is mighty fine.''

"Is Cherry hesitant to sell?"

"I'm not sure why she's holding out. She's barely scraping by since Wendell passed on. She's hinted at selling the whole operation, moving away. Something keeps her here though, she's reluctant to get down to the paperwork on that bull.''

"Maybe she's waiting for you."

"Me?" He looked at her oddly.

"Maybe she's looking to have you take over more than just Casanova. Maybe she'd like to give the animal to you, along with her land and herself.''

He shook his head. "Cherry's a neighbor."

Hannah shrugged. Men could be so obtuse at times. And from what she'd seen, Cherry Peyton had her sights set on Wyatt.

"Do you *need* that bull? I mean for financial reasons?" Was her presence here going to cost him?

He tipped his hat back, propped an elbow on the open window, and navigated the road with one hand on the steering wheel. "Winters are tough on the stock. We lose a lot. Plus we had a bad run last year with disease. Added to the fluctuating beef market, and profits are slim. I'm always looking for a way to increase my bottom line.''

He hadn't actually answered her question, but she let it pass. She didn't want to embarrass him if his finances were on shaky ground.

A toucher by nature, Hannah reached across the space separating them and laid her hand on his arm. "I'm sure you'll get your bull.''

He went very still, his eyes flaring. Here was that look again, the look that literally held her with his gaze alone, so singular, so potent.

She licked her dry lips, unconsciously leaned toward him.

A high-pitched bleat distracted them both.

"What in the world?"

Wyatt slowed the truck. "Look." He pointed across the creek. "An antelope fawn."

The tiny creature was caught in the fence, its mother nervously pacing on the opposite side. "Oh, the poor thing. Can we help it?"

"Maybe." Wyatt gauged the creek and the sturdiness of the bank. Thinking he'd hit it on the high side, he did the one thing he'd told his employees never to do. He didn't get out and do a walking recon. He just put the truck in four-wheel and headed across.

When he hit the edge of the water, it dawned on him what a bouncy ride he was giving Hannah. At the last minute he let his foot off the gas, worried over her and the baby's safety, visions of early labor scaring the tar out of him. With the loss of momentum, the back tires dug in, spun. The truck walked sideways, aligned itself with a boulder.

"Damn it. Hold on." Too late to back out now, he tried making it over the rock, miscalculated, and high-centered the truck, the undercarriage teetering on the bolder.

A lot of good four-wheel drive did him when none of those wheels were touching the ground.

He nearly pounded on the steering wheel, but refrained.

Hannah, wise woman, kept silent. Although her knuckles were white on the dash, she didn't make a peep or attempt to give instructions.

He appreciated that.

He was embarrassed enough as it was.

"Well, we're in a bit of a mess."

She smiled. "Just like an amusement park ride."

He looked at her strangely for a moment, then laughed. "I like you Hannah Richmond. You're a good sport."

"So, what now?"

"Now, we have to do the unthinkable and call somebody to come get us unstuck."

"The men aren't too far from us, are they?"

"We need a vehicle with a winch. Glen's still at the ranch. But every man carries a radio. They'll all hear my call."

"I take it having to call for a tow is right up there with having to ask for directions?"

"Not that I agree with that very sexist remark, but yes, that's about the upshot of it."

She grinned at him again, reached over and squeezed his arm. Touching him was part of the reason they were in this fix in the first place.

He couldn't think clearly when Hannah touched him, when her citrus scent wrapped around him and teased his senses. When he wanted nothing more than to take her in his arms and kiss those plump lips, to skim her smooth skin, to press her against the seat and…

He snatched the radio's mike and depressed the button. "Wyatt to base. Glen are you there?"

He waited, watching the fawn that had given up the struggle and was resting in the fence, its mother licking its face as though lapping up tears.

"Skeeter here, Wyatt. What's up?"

Wyatt's back teeth snapped together. "I was calling for Glen."

"Heard you just fine. Asked you a question, though."

He closed his eyes, waited a beat. He would take some ribbing over this.

"I stuck the truck." His words were terse and spare.

The sound of bawling cows and male chuckles came over the radio. "Cute," he said.

"What?" Hannah asked.

"Skeeter just opened the mike so I could hear the rest of the guys laughing."

"Do you often laugh at one another when you get the vehicles stuck?"

"No. Just the opposite. It's the fact that *I* did it."

The radio squawked. "Glen here, boss. I'll come. Where are you?"

Wyatt gave their location, replaced the mike and opened the truck door. "I'll go see if I can free that fawn."

"Wait! You're not going to leave me here, are you?"

"The truck's not going anywhere."

"Still, I'd rather go with you. What if it falls off the rock or something?"

He smiled. It would only have a few inches or so

to drop, not like going off a cliff or anything. "Stay put. I'll come around."

Hannah was reluctant to make any big moves for fear of rocking the truck or doing something wrong. Aside from her unease over the precarious perch of the vehicle, she didn't want to just sit there. She wanted to participate. Interact with nature.

Be with Wyatt. In his world.

She didn't want to look like the city woman that she was. Darn it, she was trying. And learning.

Wyatt came around the front and opened her door. Centered on the rock this way, it was a ways to the ground—and the water in the creek.

He reached for her, lifted her down and into his arms, cradling her until they reached the bank of the creek, his boots wading through a couple inches of water and rocks.

It was a beautiful trickling creek, looking innocent, fresh, and clean. Restful. But it had certainly made a mess of the truck. The front tires were actually on the grassy bank, but the boulder under the chassis kept the truck from going anywhere.

Once on firm ground, he let her slip to her feet, the front of her body sliding down his. Erotic friction arced between them. With her arms wrapped around his neck, he paused for just an instant when their faces were level.

Eyes held. Silent questions were asked but left unanswered. Desire was evident but went unquenched.

Lips so close they could have brushed, opened slightly, breath mingling with breath. Around them, birds chattered from fence posts.

And the baby fawn bleated in distress.

Her feet touched the ground and her blood pulsed.

Assured that she was steady, Wyatt turned and strode toward the trapped antelope. She watched him go, kept a slight distance.

She didn't know if she'd ever felt such fierce desire in her life. She didn't know she was even capable of these rushing feelings, the ache, the throbbing that was like a scream building, shouting for release.

She wanted to make love with this cowboy worse than she wanted to breathe.

Heart still galloping, she watched as he gently freed the fawn from it's trap, lifting it in his arms and setting it over the fence where it bounded away to join its mother.

His hold on the small animal had been so gentle, his voice soft and soothing as he'd worked.

He stood for a moment and watched mother and baby, then turned, his gaze meeting hers across the space of several feet.

The air smelled sweet, the breeze warm. A couple of mockingbirds fussed at one another from the fence top.

Still, the tension between Hannah and Wyatt was like a tangible thing, electrifying, provocative.

She didn't know who took the first step.

She felt her feet moving, saw his intent stride match hers until the gap between them closed, faster now, as though touching were of life and death importance.

One more step and she was in his arms, his mouth

moving over hers, his arms wrapped around her, lifting her up on her toes.

He kissed her with the single-minded intent of a man with a keen thirst. Here was the intensity she'd felt earlier, the certainty that his entire attention was focused strictly on her and nothing else.

He made her feel like the only woman on the face of the planet, made her feel special and desirable and sexy.

And he made her come alive, brought out a bold self-assurance that she hadn't known she possessed.

She kissed him back with every fiber of her being, giving as much as she took, surprising a groan out of him.

His hands raced over her back, her sides, slipped under her top, cupped her breasts.

"You're so soft. You feel so good."

"Mmm," was all she could manage to reply. Her mind was wrapped up in sensations that left no room for coherent thought much less conversation.

The squawk of the radio made them both jump apart like scalded cats.

Hannah blinked as if she'd just come out of a dark tunnel into the blinding sunlight. Wyatt was breathing hard.

Wyatt cleared his throat. "That was…"

"Earth shaking."

"I was going to say inexcusable."

She looked as though he'd socked her. "Why?"

"We're supposed to be looking for suitable ranchers for you. If we keep this up, it'll only cloud both of our thinking."

Glen's voice over the radio plus the sound of an approaching vehicle put an end to the conversation.

Wyatt waded through the creek and snatched the mike.

"Go ahead, Glen."

"Sheriff's on his way."

Wyatt smothered a groan. "I see." The cruiser was kicking up dust as it came down the dirt service road. Trust Bodine to be monitoring their radio frequency on his scanner.

"Still want me to come?" Glen asked.

"Stay put until you hear from me. Cheyenne's car has a winch. He'll probably be able to get us loose."

The sight of a horse and rider racing the sheriff's car caused Wyatt to shut his eyes. Hell on fire, were they going to have a town meeting right out here in middle of the pasture? With him obviously still half-aroused?

He went to stand by Hannah as Cheyenne Bodine stopped the cruiser, and Cherry Payne reined her horse right next to him.

He did groan this time.

"What?" Hannah asked.

"It's damned embarrassing to stick the truck. It tears up the equipment and takes up everybody's time. I'm always fussing at the men, lecturing on caution, and here I go and do the very thing." Because he'd been concentrating on Hannah's touch and not on what he was doing.

Cheyenne got out of the car, leaned his arms on the top and tipped back his hat. "Afternoon Wyatt. Hear you're having some troubles." Bodine grinned and sent a charming smile in Hannah's direction. "Good to see you again, Hannah. Looks like your tour guide could use the services of the cavalry."

Wyatt scrutinized the sheriff. Tall, half-Indian, good-looking. Available. The right qualifications, he thought, his mind halfheartedly trying to conjure an image of Hannah and Cheyenne Bodine together. After all, he was supposed to be finding her a suitable husband, repairing the wrong that Ozzie had perpetuated.

Kissing her like he'd just done was *not* part of the plan. He had to remember that.

Hannah elbowed him in the ribs. "You're doing it again," she said, smiling, her lips barely moving, her voice soft enough for only his ears.

He glanced down at her. Cheyenne was by the car still, grinning at them over the top. "What?"

"Being obvious. We're going to have to change Ozzie's gang to the *five* musketeers."

Darn it all, matchmaking was *not* his thing.

"You're right. Besides, you're looking for a rancher, not a cop."

She gave him a provocative look that slammed right into his gut, flipped his heart and made him hot and hard in an instant.

This wasn't going to work. He was trying to give her away and all he could think about was taking her to bed.

THE NEXT MORNING, Hannah was up early and had fed the chickens and groomed and visited with Daisy before Ian woke up. She hadn't yet gotten up the nerve to tackle the egg gathering after the incident with the snake, but knew she was going to have to face that chore sooner or later.

Much later was her choice.

She stood outside the kitchen door staring at a stretch of soil that wasn't covered with grass.

Wyatt, already astride his horse, rode up next to her, looking down from beneath his buff-colored hat. Strong hands lightly held Tornado's reins as he leaned an elbow on the saddle horn and tipped back his hat.

Just looking at him, so tall and masculine in the saddle, gave her a giddy thrill.

"You're in awfully deep concentration about something," he said.

It was uncanny how he kept an eye out for her, always aware and watchful. It was a wonder the man could get any work done for worrying about her.

Then again, maybe it was a good thing. Perhaps he was aware because he was attracted to her. Like she was to him.

Perhaps he *wanted* to be near her, in which case, the distraction she presented in his life could well be played up.

"I was just thinking about this piece of ground here. It's going to waste and it'd make a great place for a garden. Would you mind if I...uh, got some seeds and gave it a try?"

"You can practice all you want on my ranch, remember?"

She nodded. "When Ian gets up, I'll go into town and see what I can round up."

"Check with Henry over at the feed store. In fact, I'll take you if you want."

"No. You've got work to do."

He hesitated. "Do you remember the way?"

"The one thing I'm very good at is directions." Although she'd never relied on cows and fence posts and abandoned, rusted-out tractors to mark the way.

He nodded, still watching her in a way that made her want to place her hand on his knee and tell him it would all be okay. She didn't know why she felt that way, what his look meant, what those flashes of sadness and longing were caused by.

"Do you need money?"

"No." Just like a married couple, she thought, then cautioned herself not to get carried away. "This is my project, and in case I'm totally inept at it, I want to make sure I'm the one who funds it."

"You couldn't be totally inept if you tried."

Her laughter startled a robin perched on the satellite dish. "That's the biggest white lie I've heard in a long time, but I thank you for sparing my feelings."

His brows shifted, lifting his hat, his lips curving in a slow, sexy smile that made her heart skip. "No lie, Hannah Richmond. You've got more guts and spirit and capability than any woman I know."

The compliment was genuine. She had no idea what he was basing it on, but she glowed under his praise. And she became even more determined to make her garden flourish.

HANNAH RAN INTO Cherry Peyton in the feed store. She wore jeans and a vest and a cotton shirt rolled up showing off tanned, well-defined arms. Her red hair brushed her shoulders with lush fullness. She was a beautiful woman.

And she looked at Hannah like the outsider she was.

A reluctant smile touched Cherry's lips as she noticed what Hannah was inspecting.

"A garden will take some hard work." Her gaze went to Hannah's pregnant stomach. "I don't imagine Wyatt will have the time to help you out. We're coming up on the busy season in ranching."

Although there appeared to be unavoidable competition between them, Hannah was determined to make peace with Wyatt's neighbor. After all, she was hoping to be Cherry's neighbor, too.

She smiled. "I know it seems like a crazy thing to tackle, but I've always loved the feel of earth beneath my hands. It's very soothing. And since I'm not exactly in condition to ride out and chase after cows, it'll give me something to do."

Cherry seemed about to say something, then obviously changed her mind. "I saw your little boy up at the counter talking to Henry."

"Is Henry surviving?"

"Henry always survives. Meddles almost worse than Ozzie, but he's a good man. So, how are you getting along on the ranch?"

"Truthfully? Just about every animal out there scares the devil out of me. Luckily, I'm very stubborn. I'm determined to win. The goat and I are making progress. The skunks and chicken snakes are another matter, however."

Cherry laughed, seemingly despite herself. "I'll let you in on a secret. I hate chicken snakes, too."

Hannah relaxed. "You have no idea how wonderful that makes me feel. I'm a bit in awe of you, you know."

This appeared to take the other woman aback. She recovered quick enough, glanced back at where Ian was now perched on the wooden countertop by the cash register, a lollipop bulging in his cheek.

"He looks enough like Wyatt to be family." With a sigh, Cherry took a step back. "Good luck with the garden. Watch out for the potato bugs."

Hannah wanted to know what the heck a potato bug was, but Cherry had already turned away and was hefting a very large, heavy-looking sack up to her shoulder.

Yes, there was awe. She couldn't imagine hefting sacks of feed—at least not while pregnant—but maybe some day...

"Hannah Richmond?"

Hannah turned and smiled as Ozzie Peyton rushed toward her. At this rate she'd never get her seeds purchased. But oh, it was wonderful to go into a store and actually know people.

"I thought that was you."

"Hard to miss me, seeing as I'm the only pregnant woman in town."

"And mighty pretty you look, too."

"Flatterer."

Ozzie's vivid-blue, Paul Newman eyes softened. "My Vanessa, God rest her soul, was always sayin' that to me, too."

"Oh, I'm sorry for your loss." She wondered if it was recent.

"I miss her, you bet. Wonderful woman. Was a schoolteacher. In fact, she taught Wyatt. She'd have liked you, approved. You bet."

"Would she have approved of what you did?"

Ozzie had the grace to look abashed. But only for a moment. "Yes, as a matter of fact, she did."

Hannah frowned. "She did?"

"Well, I like to think so, anyway."

Ah, Hannah thought. He still talked to his wife, kept her close in his heart. That was fine. Touching, in fact.

He looked at her, his gaze shrewd. "Do you think I made such a big mistake?"

Hannah couldn't hold his resolute stare.

"Me and the boys were right about you," he said softly. "You're just what Wyatt needs."

"So you think. That's not exactly what *he* thinks, Ozzie."

"Give him time, he'll come around."

That's what she was hoping for. But she'd hoped for things before in her life and had setbacks. It didn't stop her from trying, but at least she knew to take a realistic view.

"I'm not sorry I came, Ozzie, if that's what you're trying to find out."

"That's half the battle, then, ain't it? You're gonna be good for Shotgun Ridge. You wait and see."

"Ozzie Peyton, now what are you up to?"

At the sound of Iris Brewer's voice, Ozzie jerked around like a puppet on a string. "I'm just visiting,

Iris.'' In an exaggerated whisper to Hannah, he said, "Woman nags me more than my Vanessa did.''

"Since Vanessa was one of my dearest friends, I consider it my duty to nag you,'' Iris said as Ozzie made a comical escape toward the front of the store. She reached out a hand to Hannah. Her other hand was holding Ian's.

"I found this cherub eating candy before lunch and thought perhaps you'd join me in a burger before you leave town.''

"I'd love to. Just let me pay for these seeds and tomato plants.''

"Oh, a garden. What a lovely idea. It's very sooth-ing to work in the soil.''

"That's what I was telling Cherry a few minutes ago.'' Though it gave Hannah a punch to know that she might not be around to see it bloom.

Iris smiled. "My Becky didn't like to garden.''

Here Hannah felt uncomfortable. She wasn't sure how to respond. Whether to talk about Wyatt's late wife or not. But Becky had been Iris's daughter first and foremost. And that was a loss the woman would feel keenly.

"Do you think it's a bad idea that I plant one?''

"Oh, no. Mary—Wyatt's mother—always threat-ened to put one right out the back door, but she had a better way with stray animals than with plants. Al-ways preferred to get her vegetables from town. You go right ahead and plant to your heart's desire. But you make Wyatt or one of the men do the digging. That's too much for you in your condition.''

"Wyatt's got enough to do at the ranch. I don't

want to take him away from it. I'll pace myself, though, I promise."

Iris hefted Ian up in her arms, even though the boy was probably too heavy. It was clear by the way her arms wrapped around him, by the way she pressed her lips to his chubby cheeks and laughed at his squeal, that she ached for the grandson she'd lost.

She looked at Hannah, hesitated. "If you like, I can come over and help...that is, if you even want the company."

"I'd love the company, and the help. I've never had a vegetable garden. I can grow roses and azaleas like nobody's business, but I'm not sure about carrots and lettuce and such."

"Nothing to it. A little mulch and water and a loving hand and you'll have abundance in no time."

"Did I hear someone speaking about abundance?"

Hannah looked up to see the young preacher, Dan Lucas, heading toward them. My goodness, it appeared that the feed store was the meeting place for the entire town.

"I thought Brewers was the hub around here," Hannah whispered.

Iris grinned. "Folks see a familiar truck and they'll change their plans and destination just to stop in and speak. They're especially interested when they see the vehicle belongs to the new person in town.

To the pastor, Iris said, "We're talking vegetable abundance."

"Well, that's close enough. Did you tell Hannah about the town dance at your place a week from Saturday? And about the potluck after church on Sunday?'' He asked the question of Iris, but held out his hand in greeting to Hannah. ''With so many new faces showing up in town, we've got to roll out the welcome. Good to see you, Hannah.''

''Likewise.''

''I haven't gotten a chance to mention either function,'' Iris said. ''We're headed over to the saloon for lunch. Would you like to join us, Dan?''

''No. I'm due out at Lenette Turman's place. Her Doug has taken a turn for the worse.''

''Oh, no.'' To Hannah, she explained. ''Doug had a stroke a while back. Give Lenette my love, will you, Dan? And tell her I'll be by.''

''Certainly. We'll see you this Sunday, Hannah? And at the dance next week?''

''I—I guess.''

The young preacher nodded and waved. ''About time this town started hopping again.''

Ozzie, standing at the counter next to Henry nodded sagely and turned to his buddy. ''Isn't that exactly what we were sayin' Henry? Ya ask me, we done a darn smart thing here. You bet.''

Chapter Ten

When Hannah and Ian got back to the ranch, she grabbed the ice chest that held her coveted Fudgsicle pops, and got out of the truck.

"Can we eat it now, mama? Pwease?"

"Ian, you've already had a Fudgsicle on top of that huge lunch. You'll burst."

Walking up to the back door, she came to a halt. The soil on the plot of ground where she wanted to plant her garden had been turned over and rows furrowed, ready to drop seeds into.

Wyatt, shirt off, skin glistening in the afternoon sun, hat on his head, leaned on a hoe and grinned at her.

"Hey! Wyatt digged the dirt!" Ian forgot all about the Popsicles and skipped right over to investigate. There was something about boys and dirt that attracted one another.

And there was something about a man and dirt, also. Goodness, this cowboy was a sight.

She moved closer, touched by what he'd done for her, riveted by the sight of sweat trickling down his bare chest, picking up a trail of dust on its descent toward the belt at his waist.

A silver buckle rested against his washboard-flat stomach. She dared not let her eyes go any lower.

She looked up at him. "You didn't have to do this for me."

He shrugged. "I had some time."

She doubted that. "Thank you."

"No big deal." He picked up his shirt from the ground, slipped it on but didn't button the front.

Hannah decided that was even sexier. Wyatt Malone had *presence*. It was in the way he carried himself. Oh he was handsome, that went without saying. But his were more of the chiseled, classic good looks sculpted by laughter and life.

"How did you accomplish this so quickly?" she asked.

"Brought the tractor in and gave it a couple passes. So, how'd it go in town?"

"Good. I got a couple of starter plants and the seeds. Six different kinds." She held up the packages like a prize. "Seems like I talked to half the residents of Shotgun Ridge."

Wyatt smiled. "That'll happen. Usually have to allow at least forty-five extra minutes just for visiting when you make a trip to town."

"There's a dance a week from Saturday, and a pot-luck after church the next day. I told Pastor Lucas we'd be there."

His hand tightened around the handle of the hoe. Then he nodded. "What's in the ice chest?"

"Fudgsicle pops." She fiddled with the charm on

her necklace, gave a sheepish smile. "I don't know if it was a craving or a fond memory."

"Can't have cravings or memories going unfulfilled."

Ian pounced on a cricket and Wyatt snagged him, tickling him and hoisting him to his shoulder. She thought back to Cherry's comment. Man and boy did look enough alike to be related. And the way Wyatt responded to her son made everything within her go soft.

This was so good for Ian. Allan had never roughhoused with his son, never carried him on his shoulders or put him on a horse or took time to listen and answer endless questions.

The genuine attention Wyatt gave to her son, the caring, was reason enough to fall in love with him. Assuming she even needed a reason in the first place.

It was fairly obvious that he was half in love with her boy. She wondered if those feelings could extend to her.

She vowed to try everything in her power to make that so.

IT TOOK TWO DAYS to get her garden planted. There were still chores to do with housecleaning, changing the sheets on the beds, preparing meals, and taking care of the chickens, the goat and Daisy.

Hannah was pleasantly exhausted. Living on Wyatt's ranch was hard work, but it was challenging. It allowed her to be outdoors, to try new experiences, to simply gaze off in the distance and see endless miles of prairie or bright-blue sky.

The smells and sounds soothed her.

It amazed her that she could be so busy yet feel no stress. It had to be good for the baby she carried in her womb. She knew it was good for Ian. Her son was thriving in this atmosphere, in the company of Wyatt and his cowboys. They all seemed to delight in Ian's antics and questions, each man taking pride in teaching the boy something new.

Kneeling in the dirt, patting the rich soil around her seeds, her gaze alighted on something horrible at the same moment her hand came down on it.

Jerking back, an uncontrollable shriek burst from her throat and she leaped up. Shuddering, she did a little running-in-place dance, her skin crawling, never giving a thought to the picture she presented.

When she gained control of herself, she had the presence of mind to look around to see who'd witnessed her ridiculous display.

Wyatt stood a few feet away, hesitating as though he weren't sure if she'd taken leave of her senses or not.

His hazel eyes were filled with amusement, his lips curved ever so slightly. "I don't see any blood or snakes. What'd you run into?"

Another shiver tracked down her spine. Nevertheless, she straightened her shoulders. "You have prehistoric creatures in the earth."

His brows lifted, shifting the hat on his head.

"A horrible bug. It was sort of white…and it had a head. A big one. I swear it looked at me."

He chuckled. "Potato bug."

"But I didn't plant potatoes. Cherry warned me to

watch for them, so I deliberately didn't plant potatoes.''

"Don't need potatoes. They're not discriminate.''

"Now you tell me.'' She eyed the soil, gripped the
spade in her hand, and took a step back among her
neatly furrowed rows. By darn, she'd find that ugly
sucker and kill it.

It crawled over a clump of dirt and Hannah lost her
nerve, squealed again and jumped back.

Wyatt caught her when she leaped three rows in a
single bound. He was so enchanted by this woman,
he didn't quite know how to contain or compartmen-
talize his feelings.

Taking the spade from her fingers, he set her aside.
"Allow me to slay your dragons, madam.''

"You'd be better off getting the gun. That bug
should be classified as an animal.''

He laughed. Yes, definitely enchanted.

After he dispatched the nasty bug, the radio at his
belt squawked. "Hey, boss, you by the two-way?''

Wyatt took the radio from his belt and responded.
"I'm here, Trevor.''

"Got a bull on the loose. That fence on Butterhill's
down again—the one on Cherry's side. Steve and I've
been looking for a while, but there's a lot of ground
to cover.''

"I'll take the plane up. You two work on the fence
until I see if I can spot him.'' Bulls on the loose were
not good, but occasions just like this gave Wyatt a
sense of contentment and anticipation. He loved any
excuse to fly the plane.

He looked at Hannah. "How'd you and Ian like to take a ride with me?"

"More four-wheeling?"

"No." Evidently she hadn't heard the radio conversation. She was still eyeing the dirt with suspicion. "Flying."

"As in a plane?"

"The very thing." He grinned at her hesitation, her interest, saw her decision flash across her face. He loved the adventuresome side of Hannah Richmond. She might have fears, but she faced them, was always game to try something new.

It was attitudes like Hannah's that made a woman special.

Even though it didn't always make them stay.

"I'd love to," she said, pleasing him more than he wanted to admit.

THE LITTLE PIPER CUB was barely big enough for two people. With Ian in her lap, both of them strapped in, Hannah concentrated on breathing normally. She wore headphones so she could talk to Wyatt above the noise of the plane. Ian had worn himself out early with his excitement and now his head slumped against Hannah's breast.

She smoothed back his sweaty hair from his forehead.

They flew along the highway now, Wyatt pointing out his land that stretched for as far as they could see.

"I noticed the white crosses along the road," Hannah said.

She saw his hands stiffen on the yoke, but she

couldn't see his eyes behind the aviator-style sunglasses.

''The state does that where there've been accidents ...fatalities.'' He put the plane into a gentle turn, followed the ribbon of asphalt that was bordered by endless miles of prairie. ''That's Becky and Timmy's.''

She barely gazed in the direction he nodded. Instead, she reached over the top of Ian's head and pressed a hand to Wyatt's arm. ''I imagine the reminder is painful. But you could look at it as a sort of tribute to them.''

He nodded, banked the plane away, heading out across the grazing pastures, over a creek with sunny buttercups and willows growing along its banks.

''There's our runaway bull.'' He keyed the mike, gave the men his coordinates.

He buzzed the area until Trevor and Steve rode in and waved him off, indicating they'd seen the bull for themselves.

''Modern conveniences,'' Wyatt murmured. ''Makes my life easy.''

For a while they simply flew in silence, the sky so blue it nearly blinded. There were trees around Wyatt's house—planted as a windbreak by the area's first generation Malones—but other than that it was wide-open space with the unobstructed beauty of incredible sunrises, sunsets and skyscapes. As they flew east, though, the terrain changed to gently rolling hills and pine-topped ridges.

''You like this, don't you?'' Hannah said when the silence had stretched for a while. After the initial tension, it had turned into a comfortable kind of quiet.

"I love it. Even more than being on horseback."

"It must be a wonderful feeling to own all this, to know that it's yours."

"The land's been in my family for four generations. The first Malone parlayed a bull and a few heifers into a good-size cow outfit. Over the years, we've acquired more and more property. As the herd increases, so does the need for grazing land."

"And you intend to increase your herd even more with Cherry's bull."

"That's the plan."

"Wyatt?"

"Hmm?"

"Would you tell me about Becky and Timmy?"

She didn't think he was going to answer. The monotonous drone of the plane's engine filtered in the headsets. She'd brought the subject up now because somehow, it seemed that a conversation like this would be easier conducted through the impersonal radio waves via headphones. Perhaps it would make it less painful.

"It was four years ago. Timmy was a year old. A cute, bubbly one-year-old, pulling himself up on tables to stand and starting to let go." He paused, his Adam's apple working convulsively. Though he was looking out at the open sky, Hannah knew he was seeing his son and swallowing tears of grief. "I never got to see him take his first step."

Oh, the pain. It was raw in his voice, fresh, even after the passage of time. She was almost sorry she'd asked about this, tried to imagine if it had been Ian, how she would have felt. Her imagination wouldn't even go there.

She tightened her arms around her sleeping son, counting her blessings that she had him to hold.

"It was a single-car accident. We can only speculate that an animal came out in front of her. Or that she'd fallen asleep or her mind had wandered. She'd run off the road, overcorrected and lost control of the car. I spotted the wreckage from the plane, landed on the highway. But they were already gone."

"I'm so sorry," she said again. Inadequate words, but what could a person say that would ease?

His memories seemed to turn inward for a long moment. Then he spoke softly. "Becky was raised here—granted it was in town." He glanced at her for a second. "Iris and Lloyd own the saloon."

"I know."

He nodded. "Even being raised here, she was tired of it. Wanted more, but I wasn't sure what. She started making trips to Billings, buying stuff she didn't really need, I guess trying to fill a void in her life that I couldn't."

Hannah couldn't imagine Wyatt not being able to meet a woman's needs. Any woman's. "Maybe she simply thought the grass looked greener in the city?"

He shrugged. "Maybe. But isn't that the same thing you're doing? Looking for greener pastures here in the country?

"Perhaps."

"So, what makes you think you'll be content?"

"Because this is something I've wanted all my life. I didn't just wake up one morning in California and decide I was unhappy with the pace. This life-style has tempted me and intrigued me for years."

"You've idealized it. And me," he said. "You've got your heart set on the cowboy mystique, not necessarily the person."

A month ago, she might have considered that his statement had validity. Now that she'd met him, though, fallen in love, she knew it was different.

She wanted Wyatt Malone and everything that he stood for.

Oh, sure, the fantasy had been glamorized in her overactive imagination. But the reality was so much better.

She nearly told him her thoughts, but his look stopped her. A tiny corner of her mind registered that he wasn't watching the sky, that the little plane was practically flying itself. But she didn't mention that, either.

Because at that moment, he reached across the small space between them and rested his hand on her knee palm up. It was a gesture that asked for reciprocation, and she placed her hand in his. He gave a gentle squeeze.

Dark glasses hid his eyes, his expression. The headset impersonalized some of the emotion in his voice, but not all of it.

"I'm not that person, Hannah. That husband you came here for. I don't have it to give."

"Because you gave it away? To your wife?"

His incredibly broad shoulders lifted in a stiff shrug. "You might as well know the whole ugly truth. It was my fault—the accident."

"What?" She couldn't have been more stunned if he'd told her they were passing a UFO.

"I couldn't keep her happy. I wasn't willing to compromise."

"Wyatt, this ranch is your life."

"It was my father's, too, but he's in Florida right now. That's what Mom wanted, to travel for a while, and Dad was smart enough to listen."

"You're actually blaming yourself for the accident? Did you quarrel before she left?"

"No. We didn't need to. Come to think of it, we didn't even talk. Becky was lonely and depressed. I knew it and dismissed it."

He glanced at her. "That's why I would have never run an ad like Ozzie and the guys did. If I couldn't keep a woman who was raised in this life happy, how the hell could I hope to keep a city woman happy? Love doesn't conquer all."

"That's very cynical of you, Wyatt."

"Cynical but true. I lived it. I made a stab at it and I don't think I can do it again."

"I believe people can love deeply more than once." Aunt Shirley was an example. She'd loved as a young girl and lost that husband. Then she'd met Uncle Rob and loved again.

"But can it come with guarantees?"

She shook her head. "No guarantees." He was afraid of losing again. And no one but God could promise that he wouldn't.

Wyatt's obstacles were much bigger than she'd anticipated. And that, very likely, was going to break her heart.

GAUGING THE TIME difference between Montana and Alaska, Hannah fished out the phone number of where Tori was staying. After their plane ride yesterday, she realized she needed to make some contingency plans...just in case.

She had to face the possibility that her stay in Montana might not be permanent—at least here in Shotgun Ridge.

She still held out hope that it could be, but she had both Ian and her pride to think about.

And she wouldn't settle for anything less than love.

She'd been there, done that...and wouldn't do it again.

The phone rang twice on the other end.

"Tori Carrington." Groggy, with an attempt to sound alert.

"Hey, sleepyhead. Rise and shine."

A pause. "You're disgusting, do you know that? It's barely 6:00 a.m. here. What the heck time is it in California?"

"I'm not in California." Hannah looked out the kitchen window and saw Wyatt striding between the barn and the corral. "I'm in Montana."

"Oh, no. You're not at my place, are you?" There was a rustle of sheets, the snick of a lighter, an indrawn breath as Tori sucked in her morning shot of nicotine.

"No. You already told me you'd be in Alaska for the month. I thought you were going to quit smoking."

"I'm working on it. So, if you're not at my place, where are you?"

"Shotgun Ridge."

"Where the heck is that?"

Hannah smiled. "A little dot on the map a couple hours from Billings."

"And you're there because…?"

"Well…" This was the tricky part. Tori, older by two years, had always been the adventuresome one, while Hannah was the home, hearth, feet-in-the-ground, rooted one. "There was this ad—uh, in your magazine, in fact—"

"Please tell me you didn't," Tori interrupted.

"I did."

"Which issue?" More rustling now.

She pictured Tori searching through her stack of magazines. "February."

"Shotgun Ridge, Shotgun Ridge," Tori repeated like a song as the sound of pages ruffling came over the receiver. "Oh…my…goodness."

"You found it."

"I found *him*. Hannah, he's a hunk!"

"He's a really nice guy."

"So, why does he have to advertise for a bride? And what the heck were you thinking to go off like that? Answering an ad from a stranger? Why didn't you call me? Let me check him out—my gosh, it says they don't have women in this town!"

"That's a bit of an exaggeration." She could hardly keep up with her sister's rapid-fire questions.

"He misrepresented himself and his town?" Tori asked, aghast.

"No. Tori, calm down, would you?"

"That's a lot to ask, sis. In fact, I'm wondering if

I'm actually talking to my sister and not some crazy person who's inhabited her body. I mean, you didn't even know if this guy was decent. He could have been an ax murderer or something.''

"I wrote to him."

"Oh, that makes it just fine. Hunkiness aside, this Wyatt Malone could have been a serial killer."

"Tori, your imagination is running away with you. Wyatt's not a criminal or anything else."

"Just a guy who has to advertise for a mail-order bride."

"Well, that's the thing. He didn't."

Tori groaned. "I don't think I'm awake enough for this conversation."

Hannah smiled. And listening to the deep breaths coming across the telephone line as her sister smoked, she related the story from the beginning.

"Oh, that's tough that he lost his wife and little boy," Tori said.

"Yes. He's so good with Ian. And Ian is thriving here, Tori. He's hardly even stuttering anymore."

"That's great. And how about you, Hannah? Are you thriving? I know what you went through with Allan. I also know that after that fiasco, you'd never settle for anything less than love."

"I do love him," Hannah said softly.

"And?" Tori asked just as softly.

"And I think he loves my kid." She paused. "I think he *could* love me. I want to believe that there are second chances for all of us."

"Like Aunt Shirley."

"Yes." Hannah closed her fist around the crystal

heart necklace, the pendant warm from her skin. "I want what she had."

"Have you thought about what you'll do if that doesn't work out?"

"That's why I was calling. I knew you'd be on assignment for the month, and I know I should have told you my plans beforehand, but I figured if it didn't fly here, I'd come hang out with you for a bit. I'm done with my old life."

Tori was silent for a long pause. "You packed up all your stuff?"

"The important things, yes. Tori, what's wrong?"

"I wish you'd told me. I've sublet my apartment, Hannah. The documents have already been faxed back and forth and signed. The magazine has transferred me. I'm staying in Alaska."

Chapter Eleven

The sun was setting. It was that time when daylight melted into dusk, when the cicadas harmonized with the crickets and the land glowed in deep and dreamy shades, shifting and sliding, soothing the soul.

It was the time of day that Wyatt loved, when the work was done and his life and accomplishments were laid out before him.

Here in the peaceful interlude just before twilight, he stood on the back porch and surveyed the latest change in his land.

Hannah had paused at the edge of the garden, wearing another of those gauzy skirts and long sweaters in pale lavender that made her skin resemble delicately carved ivory.

The embodiment of femininity and womanhood.

She should have looked out of place on his ranch.

Instead, she looked exactly right.

She stood with her hands on her hips. He glanced down to see what made her so obviously disgusted, and noted the problem.

He stepped up behind her, put a gentle hand on her shoulder. "We better get started for the dance."

She turned, her misty-green eyes simmering. "I'm going to have rabbit stew. Just look what they've done, Wyatt." She swept her hand in a wide arc. "They've helped themselves to every one of my brand-new shoots."

"You sure it was a rabbit? Can't have you accusing the animals falsely, especially when the deer have a certain affinity for vegetable gardens."

"I'm sure. I caught him red handed and the coward took off like a shot."

"They've been known to do that," he said dryly, noting that the cowboys were all spiffed up and piling in their trucks to head for the dance. He waved and turned Hannah away from her ruined garden. "We'll just have to try again. And put up a fence next time."

She sighed. "I really wanted to get that right."

The barely discernable note of defeat surprised him. "I know," he said, his fingers tightening in comfort at her waist. She sounded so forlorn he wanted to hug her. Instead, he steered her around the corner to the truck and hollered for Ian.

The boy charged out of the house, puppies under his arms, Lady and Chinook on his heels. Wyatt grinned, headed him off. That little kid was something.

"We have to leave the dogs at home, sport."

Ian frowned, begged with his velvety brown eyes. "Pwease? They might get scared."

"Naw. Lady and Chinook'll watch out for them. Besides, they don't know how to dance."

Ian went into a gale of giggles that invited participation. "'Kay. I'll put 'em back." He whirled around so fast, the dogs' ears flapped, which caused him to giggle again. Lady and Chinook scrambled after him, all of them bounding up the stairs like wild animals.

"No running in the house," Hannah shouted after them, then shook her head. She might as well save her breath. Seeing her son happy and thriving this way did her heart good.

Feeling one of those rare moments of absolute contentment, she stood by the truck with Wyatt, waiting for Ian to return.

They were about to go to a dance. As a family.

This was so wonderful, she thought. Family time. A family date in a family town. Unlike the snakes and skunks, this *was* in her brochure of fantasies.

But wonderful as it might be, this was a new arena she was playing in. She wasn't sure what to expect and was a little nervous.

"Do I look okay?" She realized it sounded as if she were fishing for a compliment. "I mean, am I dressed properly?"

He grinned at her primly phrased question. Then his sexy gaze took a slow pass over her body, licking flames in its path. Her breath caught and held.

"You look perfect. Stunning."

That surprised a laugh from her. "Let's not go overboard."

He brushed his knuckles lightly across her cheek, moved closer. She thought he was going to kiss her. Right here out in the open. To the song of the cicadas and the spectacular setting of the sun.

As the sky burst with vivid colors her insides did the same. Her blood went from simmer to burn in two seconds flat. She leaned toward him, already imagining the taste of him, the feel of him.

The slamming of the screen door made her jump.

Wyatt reached around her, yanked opened the truck's door.

She frowned. He almost looked angry. Then she realized what was bugging him. They'd nearly kissed. And they were on their way to a town dance where he had every misguided intention of matching her up with a suitable rancher. Despite their heated kisses, he hadn't given up on that ridiculous goal.

Hannah figured she needed a strategy to change this man's mind.

OZZIE AND LLOYD surveyed the crowd at Brewer's Saloon, well pleased. Henry and Vern came to stand beside them.

"Just look what we've done," Ozzie said proudly, noting the placement of tables around a dance floor where a nice combo was playing country tunes. "When's the last time you saw this many people in town? Any of you?"

"Been a while, that's for sure," Henry said. "It's too early to impact my feed business, but Lloyd here's going through a lot of booze and beef, and Vern's turning a pretty good dollar at the general store."

"Sure is keeping Vera hopping. Why, I even ordered a couple varieties of cigars," Vern said. "Durndest thing. Womenfolk asking for them as much as the men."

"I'll have to section off a cigar room," Lloyd said.

"You bet." Ozzie beamed, already imagining it. "I tell you this sight does my heart proud. Just wish my Vanessa was here to see it."

The four men shared a moment of silence, nodding. "Heard the widows Bagley have turned their white clapboard into a boardinghouse."

"Pretty enterprising of them," Henry commented. "Seeing as how Lloyd's place here is full up."

"Not a single vacancy," Lloyd agreed, filling four mugs with beer on tap and passing the tray to Maedean. He'd already hired himself two new waitresses for tonight. Women new to town. The direct result of their advertisements in the city papers.

"Shotgun Ridge's coming back to life, boys," Ozzie said. He smiled, nodded toward the door. "And lookie who just showed up. Our first family." He glanced at Lloyd. "You sure you're okay with this, my friend?"

Lloyd nodded. "We've been through this before and I said I was. Wyatt's a decent man. He did right by my Becky and he deserves a second chance."

"'Spect we'll have some trouble convincing him before it's all said and done."

"That Hannah'll win him over," Henry said. "Sweetest thing. Was in my store buying seeds for a garden a week ago."

"Well of course she was," Ozzie said shortly. Honestly, sometimes he wondered if his pal was having trouble in the remembering department. "I was right there and spoke to her myself. Uh-oh."

"What?" Lloyd, Henry and Vern chimed.

"Ethan Callahan at two o'clock." He pointed, all but rubbing his hands together. "And just notice the look on Wyatt's face, would you? Couldn't have timed that better if we'd planned it ourselves. Just what the boy needs. You bet. A bit of competition to put a claim on his property. He'll tumble yet. You bet."

"HEY, THERE, California. You're looking especially delightful tonight."

Strategy, Hannah thought as she returned Ethan Callahan's friendly smile. She hadn't known just what her angle would be. It hit her like a brick when Ethan turned up his innate, perfectly harmless charm.

From the corner of her eye she saw Wyatt scowl. Oh, yes. This would be good.

"Why thank you, Ethan. You clean up pretty good yourself."

Ethan gave a barely noticeable jolt, then recovered quickly enough, his eyes smiling as he caught on.

Wyatt snorted.

"Did you say something, Wyatt?" Hannah asked.

He glared and Ethan grinned. "Mind if I steal your date for a quick turn across the floor?"

"Hell, Callahan, we haven't even eaten yet. For that matter, we've hardly crossed the threshold."

"Nothing says you can't have a dance on an empty stomach. Work up an appetite."

He whisked Hannah away and Wyatt didn't have the right to stop him. And why would he, anyway? Even if she were his, which she wasn't, there wasn't a thing wrong with her dancing with another man. Becky had danced with Ethan numerous times.

He pried his eyes away from Hannah and Ethan. "Well, sport," he said to Ian. "Looks like it's you and me. What do you say we go check out the menu?"

Ian nodded happily and slipped his hand in Wyatt's. He felt the familiar softening around his heart and his chest puffed out. You didn't see Hannah's son rushing to hang all over Ethan. No, sir. It was Wyatt's hand that the boy held. And that gave him a leg up on his friend.

This crazy line of thinking disgusted him. What the heck was the matter with him? And by God, Ethan was holding Hannah too close. He took a step in that direction, nearly mowed down Ian.

"Hey," the little boy chirped.

"Sorry."

Obviously not injured, Ian tugged at Wyatt's hand and swung around as though Wyatt were a Maypole. "Nikki's here! Can I go play wif her, Wyatt?"

From across the room, Nikki was waving her arm like a baton twirler in a parade.

"Abandoning me already?"

Ian giggled. "Yep."

"Okay. Go play. But not under the tablecloths," he admonished, remembering the near fiasco at the church get-together.

Ian hesitated. "You be okay?"

"I'll be okay." God, his heart muscles were getting a workout.

The boy skipped off, leaving Wyatt alone in the

middle of a crowd, his jealous gaze once more drawn to the dance floor. A brunette he didn't recognize walked past him, blocking his view, and glanced back over her shoulder in a look that nearly shouted she was available.

Wyatt wasn't interested.

Moody, brooding, he went to the bar and ordered a beer.

Lloyd spoke, but Wyatt ignored him. He didn't trust himself to be civil right now. And that annoyed him. He was never rude to his friends.

Nursing the beer, he watched Ethan pass Hannah off to his brother, Clay. A survey of the room told him the other Callahan brother, Grant, was waiting in the wings with very little patience and a whole lot of intent.

For crying out loud. You'd think these cowboys had never seen a woman before. And for that matter, he thought as he continued his perusal of the room before his gaze was drawn back, again, to Hannah, there were considerably more women here tonight than usual.

Unfamiliar women.

He swiveled on the bar stool, not surprised to see Ozzie, Vern and Henry had joined Lloyd behind the bar and that all four old men were studying him like a steer in a 4-H project.

"What?" he snapped.

Ozzie's vivid-blue eyes twinkled even as his steely gray brows winged up. "Just thought maybe you'd want to thank us."

Wyatt's temper, normally very controlled, flashed

like a whip, singeing the air around him. The scalding emotion took him by surprise.

Their ads were responsible for the female population explosion in the town.

They were responsible for Hannah and her cute kid and that sweet baby girl that kicked and tumbled in her stomach being here.

People didn't just spring a potential wife on a man without warning. Especially a man who didn't *want* a wife. It put him in the awful position of causing hurt to that woman. Or the equally impossible position of trying to find her a suitable man to treat her right. Like she needed to be treated. Like she deserved to be treated.

Much better than anything he had to give, that he was capable of giving.

He passed a hand down his face, looked at the four men. "Why did you meddle? How can you play with people's lives this way?"

"Now, Wyatt—"

"Didn't it ever occur to you all that I'm alone for a reason? That I'm perfectly happy this way?"

"If you're so happy, how come you're snarling like a coyote over a carcass?"

"Because I've protected myself from pain these past four years and now you've slit me wide-open for it." He pushed off the stool and headed for the food table. He hadn't meant to impart that much information. The vulnerability would only encourage the old goats—sadistic souls that they were.

Grant Callahan was now twirling Hannah across

the floor, flirting and charming, having snatched her right out from under his brother, Clay's hold.

Wyatt probably ought to put a stop to it. She was pregnant, for crying out loud. She needed a rest.

He nearly started in that direction, then realized that if he took her in his arms, just the two of them, body to body, he might lose the tenuous control he held himself under.

He filled a plate with food and sat down at Stony Stratton's table. Carlotta—Lottie to her friends—and her husband Ray sat with them. Lottie was Stony's housekeeper and took care of Nikki when Stony was out working his magic on Montana's finest horses—and some that weren't so fine.

"Stratton," Wyatt acknowledged. "Lottie and Ray. How are you?"

"Oh, we're just wonderful," Lottie said with a tinkling laugh that made her sound like a girl of twenty instead of sixty. "And Nikki's in heaven having a playmate. That little Ian is a delight."

Just then, the children raced up, Ian climbing right up on Wyatt's lap as though he were a handy obstacle course.

Wyatt steadied his plate. "Whoa there, little buddy." His silky hair stuck to his sweaty forehead. "Why don't you slow down and have something to eat?"

Ian snatched a carrot off Wyatt's plate and crunched, his tiny, square white teeth oozing orange as he giggled. "I'm a rabbit."

"Best not mention rabbits around your mama. She's pretty sore at those creatures right now."

"How come?"

"They ate her garden."

"Bad."

"Yep. Pretty bad." He held out his burger and Ian took a healthy bite, dripping ketchup down his chin. Wyatt caught the sauce with a napkin.

"Want a bite?" Ian cribbed a carrot off Wyatt's plate and held it out to Nikki. "We could be bad rabbits and not tell mama."

Nikki seemed to think that was a grand idea, and Ian, obviously operating on some sort of kid signal, scrambled down from Wyatt's lap and joined the little girl in a hopping spree, their hands at their heads like floppy ears.

The scar on the side of Stony's face creased as he smiled at the kids' antics. "Those two'll never settle down tonight."

"Probably not," Wyatt agreed absently, his heart suddenly ramming against his ribs as Hannah came up to their table, her porcelain cheeks flushed, her misty-green eyes gleaming. Happiness radiated from her like the brightest star in the sky.

Jealousy slammed into him as he wondered which man had put that glow there.

Clay Callahan had snagged the brunette with the come-and-get-me eyes, and Grant was on the dance floor, plastered against a tall willow of a woman in a tight pair of jeans.

Ethan Callahan was right behind Hannah, his hand resting at her shoulder. The look she tossed the play-boy set Wyatt's blood to sizzle.

He stood, grabbed a chair and pulled it up next to

his. "Sit." With very little finesse and quite a lot of possessiveness, he tugged her down beside him.

Ethan and Stony both raised their brows. Wyatt ignored them.

"I can't remember when I've danced so much," Hannah said, her voice breathless and joyful. She picked up Wyatt's soda and took a drink. The intimacy of that action captivated him for the space of two heartbeats.

"You should have a care for you condition." He edged his plate toward her, and in case she didn't get the message, he held out his burger and urged her to take a bite. It was turning into a community burger. He, Ian, and now Hannah had all eaten off it.

"Oh, Lloyd does make the best cheeseburgers." She tried to catch a drip of mayonnaise with the back of her hand, but Wyatt's thumb was already there, taking care of it himself.

Arrested, her green eyes fastened on to his. Their knees pressed beneath the table and the room became pleasantly hazy, shrinking in to shroud them in an intimacy that excluded the rest of the occupants of the table.

Slowly, Wyatt raised his thumb to his mouth. Licked.

Hannah drew in a breath. She'd been hot from the exertion of dancing. Now she was burning from the incendiary look of this sexy cowboy.

"Well," she said at last, her mind wiped clean of witty words. "Um, thank you."

"My pleasure."

Her brows raised in a silent question. Was this a

game? He looked as confused as she felt and glanced away.

So did Hannah—and met Ethan Callahan's knowing look. On the dance floor she'd taken the playboy cowboy's measure, realized he had a marshmallow heart, an unbending sense of honor and loyalty and a sharp antenna when it came to his friends. During the short span of a dance, he'd coaxed her into spilling her guts—she was still a little surprised that he'd accomplished that feat. But she was extremely glad that he had.

Because Ethan Callahan, Shotgun Ridge's wealthiest, most eligible cowboy bachelor, had agreed to become her ally. It would be his extreme pleasure, he'd told her, to embark on a mission to help Hannah have her heart's desire.

Wyatt Malone.

"Whoa," Stony said, starting to rise. "Bunnies running amuck by the desserts."

"Bunnies?" Hannah asked, confused, upset all over again at the reminder of what rabbits had done to her garden.

"Now you've done it," Wyatt said to Stony. "We weren't supposed to say that word. I'll get the kids."

He rose and strode across the room, his stride purposeful and loose-hipped. Snaking an arm around each child, he scooped them into his arms and shuffled onto the dance floor, smoothly stepping around the floor with both giggling children's spindly arms wrapped around his neck, nearly knocking his hat off his head.

Hannah smiled and sighed. There was nothing more masculine than a man who enjoyed children.

"Well, Miss Lottie," Ray said to his wife. "Care to take a turn around the floor with an old man?"

"Don't mind if I do." They moved to the dance floor, took Nikki from Wyatt and danced with her between them.

Wyatt looked across the room, his gaze colliding with Hannah's. The sight of him holding her son, enjoying him, raised a lump in her throat.

He held out his arm in an arc, a silent invitation for her to join their circle. A family circle.

"Go, California," Ethan said. "Fill him up before he realizes he's fighting a losing battle."

She barely heard Ethan's words. Her feet moved across the floor as though silent wings carried her.

Wyatt's arm closed around her, drew her in.

"We danced like rab—people," Ian finished on a giggle.

"I see," Hannah said, closing her arm around her son, her hand coming to rest on Wyatt's wide shoulder.

He was still gazing at her with another of those exclusive looks that made her sizzle, made the room close in on just the two of them.

The *four* of them, she amended when Ian fussed with her hair and the baby in her womb shifted and tumbled.

Iris Brewer broke the spell when she came up and held her arms out to Ian.

"Mind if I cut in with this handsome young man?"

They passed Ian into her arms and she danced away

with him, Ian's delighted giggle following in their wake.

"He's so happy," Hannah said.

"As he should be. He's four."

Her smile was soft, a little sad around the edges. "He hasn't always been this way."

"He's stuttering less."

"I know."

Wyatt drew her closer, inhaling her citrus scent. "I've wanted to get you in my arms all night."

She looked up at him with those misty-green eyes, and without an ounce of guile said, "I know."

That admission, that he was so transparent, should have annoyed him. Instead, it heated his blood. She fit him like a glove. "I'm not doing my duty."

"To heck with your duty, Wyatt. Shut up and dance with me."

His smile was slow and delighted, his body aroused. "Yes ma'am." He took her through a series of smooth intricate steps that she followed like a practiced partner, as though she were one with him.

He pressed his cheek against her temple, turned slightly and brushed his lips against her hair, a butterfly caress that she wouldn't feel. Her hair smelled of lemons, her skin was so warm, her hand soft where it rested in his. He longed to tip her chin up, press his lips to that incredible mouth, feel those plump lips mold to his, the shy hesitation before they'd open.

He realized his heart was knocking brutally against his ribs, and his body was rock-hard. The music ended much sooner than he was ready. He didn't want to let her go.

They stood there in the middle of the dance floor, people having to move around them like a herd splitting for a downed calf.

Hannah cleared her throat. "Well. We'd best sit down. Cool off a bit."

He tipped his head, his hat shading the light that danced over her skin. With his hand at her waist, he guided her back to their table.

Ian and Nikki were a sight with chocolate ringing their mouths. Hannah automatically reached for a napkin and swiped.

"The children play so well together," Lottie said. "Why don't you let us take Ian home for a sleep-over?"

"Yeah!" Ian and Nikki chimed together.

"Oh, I don't know. He doesn't have pajamas. Extra clothes."

"That's no problem. I'll just wash up what he's got on and it'll be fine for church tomorrow. You all are coming to services aren't you?"

"Yes, but—"

"Then it's settled," Lottie said.

Hannah knew she was outnumbered. And it would be wonderful for Ian. He'd never been to a sleep-over before. She looked at Stony, made one last attempt. "Are you sure it's all right?"

The big, quiet man nodded. "We'd be happy to have him."

She looked at Wyatt. He nodded and she acquiesced.

They ate their dessert and the band came back from their break, strumming a familiar ballad.

Lottie, Ray and Stony stood and gathered the kids. "Best get the young ones home," Stony said in the quiet, soothing voice that made him famous because of its uncanny effect on horses. "Say good night to your mom, Ian."

Ian hopped around the table and kissed Hannah and gave her a fierce hug, then treated Wyatt to the same before racing off after Nikki.

Ethan laid down his fork. "What do you say, California? The kids are gone. It's just us consenting adults. We gonna let this slow, kissing and munching tune go to waste?"

"No," Wyatt answered for her. "We're not. So go find your own woman to nibble on."

He pulled Hannah to her feet and had her in his arms and on the dance floor all in one swoop.

Her head spun. Over Wyatt's wide shoulder, she saw Ethan wink and had to bite her lip to keep from grinning.

"I'm not used to this jealous side of you."

He glanced down at her, his eyes burning. "You should probably be quiet for a minute."

"Why?"

"Because I need a minute to concentrate. Otherwise I'm going to kiss you in a way that'll set the town to talking for a good long time—and make you forget all about Ethan Callahan."

She smiled softly, cupped her hand around his neck. "Consider him forgotten."

He made a growling sound in the back of his throat. "Hannah, I'm trying to remember my good intentions here."

"I'm not interested in your good intentions right now. Like Ethan said, we're consenting adults." She'd never in her life said anything so bold as she was about to say. She leaned back, looked directly into Wyatt Malone's eyes.

"I want you."

Chapter Twelve

The ride home was thick with a silence that was anything but comfortable. Hannah had a good half hour to vividly imagine every scenario possible that involved herself and Wyatt.

They would make love. If they didn't—if he changed his mind, found his good intentions between town and home—she would die.

She didn't know if it was baby hormones or what that made her so sensitive to him. Just sitting in the cab of the truck, smelling his masculine scent, staring at his broad shoulders, his hat brushing the headliner of the truck, his capable hands handling the vehicle with skill and ease made her ache.

His features were tight, yet every time he looked at her his eyes burned, held a promise, however reluctant.

He wanted her, but he didn't want to.

Hannah desperately wanted to push him—*had* pushed him—and that impetuous boldness still stunned. But something deep inside told her intimacy would tell one way or the other. It would bring them together or tear them apart.

The second option frightened her, nearly made her lose her nerve. But desire and optimism drove her on.

Chinook met them at the back door, tail wagging. It seemed strange without Ian there. The hushed expectancy hung heavy in the air, in every breath they took.

A light over the stove glowed softly.

He still wore his hat—as he had all night. She rarely saw him without the buff-colored Stetson. It was as much a part of him as the shirt that stretched across his broad shoulders and jeans that gloved his muscular thighs.

Nerves gripped her as the intensity of his gaze never wavered from her face. Should she make the first move? Hadn't she already done that? Seduction was new to her. She'd never considered herself good at it.

But Wyatt Malone made her feel like a woman.

When the sexual tension in the room became thick enough to cut and he still hadn't made a move to close the distance between them, Hannah's courage faltered a bit.

"Wyatt?"

"My mind tells me this isn't a good idea. My body's saying otherwise."

And your heart? She didn't ask the question. "My body's in agreement with yours."

"This wasn't what we'd agreed on."

Which time? She'd come here believing this was

exactly what they'd agreed on. But since he hadn't been the one to place that ad, that changed the rules.

She shook her head, her voice soft. "I'm a big girl, Wyatt, and I can make my own decisions. I don't need or want you to find me a husband. I'm attracted to you, and…I'm fairly certain you're attracted to me."

"You know I am."

"Then what's the problem?"

"I can't give you the promises you need. And that's not fair."

"I'm not asking for promises or fair right now, Wyatt. I just want you to put out the fire." She kept astonishing herself with the words that tumbled out of her mouth. "We agreed I'd stay until my sister got back—for the month. We have time." More than he knew, but she kept that to herself.

The emotions welling in her were almost too much to bear.

"Be sure." His voice was deep and soft, raw with desire and barely checked control. "If I touch you, if I kiss you, I'm not going to want to stop."

She licked her lips. Took a step. "I don't want you to stop."

It was all the invitation he needed. His arms were sure and strong as they came around her, his mouth claiming control of hers. It was a kiss that went from simmer to boil in less time than it took to blink.

He swept her up in his arms, the old-fashioned gallantry surprising her, arousing her. His strength was amazing, thrilling. Even with the weight of her body, he took the stairs two at a time and never even appeared winded.

This man was a fantasy come true.

"I want to go slow," he murmured. "Savor. But I'm not sure I can. Not the first time."

He didn't seem aware that he admitted there would be a next time between them. It gave Hannah hope. Incredible hope. And her love for him grew to proportions that she didn't know how to contain.

But she had to. She didn't want to scare him away.

"Then don't go slow, Wyatt. I want you now. Fast."

Her words inflamed him. With quick and clever hands, he undressed them both, eased her down against the mattress and followed her there.

But as much as he'd led her to believe this would be a fast and wild coupling, it was anything but.

His body fitted to hers with an arousing press in all the right places, yet he held his weight off her, drew her slightly to her side, cupped her face between his hands and kissed her.

Just that. Just a kiss. A kiss that was soft and warm and deep and incredibly erotic. A kiss that inflamed while at the same time sent butterfly wings battering against her stomach. A kiss that made her throb. A kiss that made her want to weep.

With his lips alone, he worshiped her, made her feel cherished and alive, both subdued and wild.

She nearly lost her concentration when he nibbled his way down her neck, over her swollen breasts. She came out of the euphoria long enough to realize that nerves were crowding in her throat, that she had a reservation or two about her body. She was pregnant, and she wasn't a young girl.

He lifted his head. "I've lost you."

This man was so perceptive. It proved that he thought of only her, focused his entire being on only her. It was a gift worth more than he'd ever know.

"I want to be beautiful for you. Sexy."

"Ah, sweetheart, you are."

"I'm not a hard-body." At five months along, she wasn't huge, but there was a definite distention.

"You're so much better." He framed her tummy with gentle palms and pressed a reverent kiss there. The emotions that welled took him by surprise. He couldn't believe how much he wished that the baby girl in her womb were his child.

He ran his hands softly over her from head to foot, arousing her by slow degrees, determined to fill her with desire so deep and fierce she wouldn't have the energy to think about curvaceous bodies.

He'd never taken more care with a woman. Not even Becky. He didn't understand why Hannah was so different, why she inspired this slow, practiced touch. It became vitally important to show her pleasure, all there was to offer.

She'd told him she hadn't been kissed in years. It became his sole mission to make up for that inexcusable lack, to sip from her sweet body, to leave not an inch of her remarkably soft skin untouched.

When his lips closed over her in the most intimate kiss a man could give a woman, she came undone.

He watched the pleasure flash across her face,

heard her surprise and satisfaction in the hoarse, ragged voice as she called his name.

"I'm right here, sweetheart."

She sucked in a breath, trembled. "We agreed on fast."

"Mmm. I changed the rules."

"You're good at that." Her words ended on a delighted gasp when his hands closed over her breasts, his mouth trailing back up her body.

Her hands roamed over his hair, his back, fingers dancing over skin, driving him mad.

"I want to touch you—more of you," she said.

"Next time. Hold on to me now." He shifted her, entered her, slowly, carefully, thoroughly.

Her breath hitched, sighed.

He filled her up, her body, her soul and her heart. It was on the tip of her tongue to tell him she loved him, but her mind was swept clean of thought when he began to move.

The friction was exquisite, a slow building wave of pleasure gathering steam until it became like a roar in her head. She was burning up. The single-minded attention he showered over her body blurred her vision, her mind.

And all the while, he watched her, gauged her pleasure, gave her more, then incredibly, even more. She couldn't even define what that 'more' was. She only knew that it was shattering.

She wanted to plead, but didn't know what to plead for. She needed, yet feared that need. It was too much. Too powerful. Too close to the coveted dream she wanted desperately to grab and hold.

He went still, buried deep inside her. She felt him throb, felt her own body synchronizing with his, the rhythm. Sensations inflamed, yet something remained elusive.

He eased back, holding her with his gaze. So still, so exquisitely erotic.

There was no wild rush for completion. He was making love to her with his mind and his body and his soul, letting her know they had all night, that he would wait for her, that he would give her the moon and take her to heaven, no matter how long it took.

Unaccountably, tears crowded her throat, emotions so huge she didn't know what to do with them. *Please,* was all she could think.

His lips lowered, barely touching, breath mingling, eyes wide-open.

And then he thrust, long and deep and Hannah nearly wept.

"Let go for me."

She wanted to. She desperately wanted to. But the feelings flooding her were new and frightening. They were too much, not enough. She felt a scream well, pound through her, never materialize. She thought she'd go mad. She was terribly afraid she'd shatter, that she'd never find the pieces of herself again.

"Let go, sweetheart. I'll catch you." His teeth clenched as he held viciously to his control. He saw the flush spread over her breasts and neck, saw her surrender, felt the spasms building, trembling on a fine precipice, tumbling.

He linked their hands and drew them up beside her head, held her gaze for a long moment, then pressed his lips to hers and swallowed her scream of completion with a kiss that rocked his soul.

In his determination to give to her, he'd miscalculated. And now, he was holding on to his heart for dear life.

WHEN HANNAH WOKE, she was alone in Wyatt's bed. She sighed and rolled over, the cool, crisp sheets feeling incredibly decadent against her naked skin.

He'd reached for her again during the night, made love to her in another one of those slow, incredibly giving sessions. His generosity and skill gave her confidence in herself once more, made her feel like a desirable, sexy woman, etched memories that would last a lifetime.

But now, in the light of day, she imagined he would feel guilt. He was a man who'd once believed in commitment, yet didn't any more.

And because he wasn't willing or able to offer that, he would have morning-after regrets.

She would have to ease that burden for him. She still had hope that he could fall in love with her. But they needed an unencumbered field in which to play. No pressure.

And if it didn't work, it wouldn't be for lack of trying on her part.

Because somewhere between last night and this morning, somewhere in the feelings Wyatt had wrung from her, the exquisite liberation, she'd realized a few things about herself.

She hadn't actually come to Montana looking for a husband.

She'd come to find herself.

The revelation had rocked her right down to her toes.

Without realizing it, she'd become wife, mother and social secretary to Allan. She'd put everyone's needs before her own.

Allan had wanted an ornament and that's what she'd tried to be. Even in sex, *she'd* been the one to give the most, as if her pleasure wasn't as important as his.

And when Ian came along, things changed. Hannah had found herself working even harder to be who Allan wanted. To be perfect.

She didn't know when *she* had stopped mattering. When she'd become a shell.

Yes, she did.

It was when she'd seen Wyatt's eyes in the mail-order bride advertisement. Just that simply, those eyes had spoken to her, had sparked the coveted memories she'd kept buried in the back of her mind for years.

Oh, she still aspired to be a wife. That wasn't the problem. Making family your career was a noble goal, an important one.

But she wanted to be an equal partner.

She wanted to feel a sense of accomplishment at the end of the day. Tired, perhaps, but fulfilled.

All the things Wyatt's ad had promised.

With Allan, she'd been suffocating in a cement grave without a personalized marker. She'd lost sight of her purpose, her pride and her identification.

She wanted more.

She wanted to matter.

"MAN ALIVE, look at the people," Wyatt said as he pulled the truck to a stop in the church parking lot. He hadn't quite known what to say to Hannah on their drive to town this morning. Their relationship had shifted, and he wasn't sure how to proceed. "Dan's going to be a happy preacher with this flock to minister to. Were all these people at the dance last night?"

"All these women, you mean?" Hannah asked, her smile soft, her green eyes full of spunk.

"The ratio's definitely tipping. I wonder how many papers the old geezers advertised in." The small talk felt stilted, inane. He should be addressing what had happened between them last night. The cinnamon scent of the apple pies Hannah had baked for the potluck filled the truck, teasing his senses.

She reached across the cab of the truck and laid a hand on his forearm, gave a gentle squeeze. "Please don't feel uncomfortable with me. Don't be sorry."

"I took advantage."

"No, if anyone took advantage, it was me. Let's just let it be, Wyatt. We have time."

Time. Wyatt made a quick mental calculation. She'd been here a little over two weeks, had less than two more to go before their time was up, before she'd go to her sister's in Billings. She was giving him permission to not think about it. To just enjoy. Permission to keep the rules just as they were, without recriminations.

And God help him, he wanted to take that time.

He got out of the truck, came around and opened Hannah's door for her, feeling manly when she gave him one of those looks that let him know he continued to surprise her.

He wanted to give her more surprises.

"Wyatt!"

The sound of Ian's voice had him turning, opening that secret place in his heart he kept well guarded. The little boy streaked across the churchyard and Wyatt grinned, striding forward to meet him halfway.

Hannah watched Wyatt hoist her son in the air, catch him up in a hug and perch him on his broad shoulder.

"Come on, Mama!" Ian shouted, wiggling and beckoning.

Both man and boy were grinning at her, inviting her into their circle. Just like last night at the dance.

She loved how this man adored her son.

With his hand at her back and Ian still riding his shoulder, he led them into the church and started to slip into the back row.

"No," Ian admonished. "Up there wif Nikki."

"We better move closer," Hannah said. "Remember what Pastor Lucas said about hiding in the back? I wouldn't put it past him to call attention in front of everybody and make us move."

Wyatt sighed, but it was a good-natured sound. "You're right. All these changes. Next thing I'll be expected to wear a tie."

Hannah snagged his hat off his head. "Your neck's safe, but the hat's another matter."

"Woman, a man's hat is sacred."

"Yeah, well, let it be sacred in your lap for a while."

He winked, allowed her to keep the hat.

They were just like a true family, walking up the center aisle of the church, teasing, nagging and glowing as though they'd found the secret of harnessing the sun.

Ozzie beamed at them as they passed, and Ethan blew her a kiss—a deliberate attempt to annoy Wyatt.

It worked. Wyatt scowled and possessively tightened his arm around her, drew her closer to his side.

Hannah had to bite her lip to keep from laughing out loud. It was Sunday morning, the sun was shining and the pansies were blooming. Hope was in the air.

Pastor Lucas was indeed in his glory and it took twice as long to introduce all the new guests, and even longer to deliver his sermon. He'd obviously felt quantity as well as quality was called for with the larger crowd. So many more souls to nurture and save.

After the services, Hannah left Wyatt to go help the ladies set up the food in the church hall. The ambiance and community spirit was vibrant and alive.

Mounds of Iris's potato salad and trays of fried chicken and ham weighed down the banquet table. Another table was set up with punch, coffee, cookies and desserts.

Hannah just stood and surveyed her surroundings, feeling a part of it all, accepted.

Feeling as though she mattered.

''That's just what I like to see,'' Ozzie said, plucking a cookie off the table beside her. ''A pretty woman with a big, happy smile. You bet.''

"Afternoon, Ozzie. You're looking pretty happy and proud yourself."

"Me and the boys love it when a plan comes together. This here's a good town. We gotta take care of it."

"Have you lived here all your life?"

"Yep. Born and raised. Married my sweet Vanessa and made a home here. We weren't blessed with children, but Vanessa was a schoolteacher. Taught pretty near every young person in town. Sort of adopted them all, treated them like her own."

"Then you had a very large family indeed."

"You bet. Family and friendships. They're important. Just kills my soul when somebody leaves, looking for greener grass."

"Like Wyatt's parents?"

"Well now, that's a different story. They stayed, raised a family and cows, and they're not truly gone. Wyatt's daddy is a great cattleman, but there's a tiny piece of his heart that yearns for adventure. Guess that's why he hightailed it off in that motor home. Now Wyatt, on the other hand, is wholehearted cowboy. Like his gramps was, God rest his soul. Won't see him up and leave. No sir. His feet are planted real firm in Montana's soil."

And that caused him guilt, Hannah knew. He felt if he'd been a little more like his father, more willing to compromise, then Becky wouldn't have made so many trips to the city, might even be alive today.

It was that guilt, that fear that kept him from giving a commitment.

And Hannah had less than two weeks to see if things could change.

Chapter Thirteen

Standing in her garden, hoe in her hand, Hannah smiled as she watched Ian frolic with the puppies in the yard. They were growing and thriving. Just like her son. Just like her garden now that Wyatt had fenced it in to keep out the rabbits and deer.

Butterflies took flight in her stomach when Wyatt saw her and came toward her. The sight of him never failed to arouse her, fill her with emotions that pushed at the seams of her heart and soul.

It was moments like these that she felt all was right with her world, viewed all she looked upon as hers.

Over the past few days, Wyatt and Hannah had discussed everything from movies to politics. They'd talked about childhood, adulthood and everything in between. In less than a month, he knew more about her than Allan had in six years.

Wyatt listened. He cared.

He'd become her friend as well as her lover.

And they both avoided the calendar.

He stopped in front of her now, ran a finger down

her nose in a gesture that was both friendly and intimate.

"You should be wearing a hat. You're going to burn that delicate skin."

"I've got on sunscreen. Who's that coming in the truck?" An old pickup with a trailer attached was whipping up a cloud of dust as it came down the drive toward the barn.

"The fellow who's picking up the llama."

"You're getting rid of Fancy?"

"She's not really ours. We've only been boarding her for Clyde Davis. His barn burned a while back. We helped him rebuild, but it's taken him a while to get back up to speed."

"Oh, in that case, this marks a happy occasion. It means your neighbor is back to normal."

Wyatt chuckled. "You make a good point."

"Mind if I tag along and say goodbye? I feel a little guilty that I never got to know Fancy. I meant to, but..." Well, she was taking it slow. One animal at a time. And there was something about that llama's eyes—cute as they were—that gave her the impression it saw too much, that it had deep thoughts and just might like to play a few tricks on her. There was no reason for her to feel that way, but she had.

Still carrying her hoe, she leaned it up against the shade of the barn as the llama and her baby were herded into the truck.

Wyatt shook hands with Davis and refused to take any money for board. Davis accepted with grace and gratitude.

"Your mother will miss her," she said when Wyatt stepped back to watch the truck pull away.

"Ha. She was the first to offer to take the thing home, then took off to see the country. But you're right. She misses all the animals. Which reminds me, we ought to butcher a couple of the chickens and put them in the freezer. The flock is getting a little large."

"My chickens?" Horrified, she sputtered, "You want to..." It didn't bear saying. "Oh, Wyatt, I'm not sure about that. How can you eat something that has a name?"

He stared at her for a minute, then roared with laughter.

Hannah might have laughed right along with him, but movement caught her eye.

Oh, God.

Snake.

Coming right up behind Wyatt. Moving slowly. Rattles glistening silver. Curling and stretching, it inched forward, directly toward him, his left boot in its path.

And he didn't see it.

She wanted to scream, but no words would come out. Adrenaline pumping, her mind went numb as instinct and fierce love took over, lent her strength, courage. She didn't remember grabbing the hoe, didn't remember shoving Wyatt to the side.

The scream trapped in her throat became a moan as she viciously hacked and hacked and hacked. For how long, she didn't know.

Wyatt grabbed the hoe on an upward swing.

Hannah went still. The blisters on her hands wept against the handle of the hoe.

The snake was a bloody mess at her feet.

Her vision still hazed, she turned and buried her face in Wyatt's neck, held him close and tight with arms that felt like rubber.

Horrible scenarios flipped through her mind. Waking nightmares her mother used to call them.

Over and over, she could see the snake striking, fangs sinking in, Wyatt's leg swelling, the distance between here and town too far. His life draining away from him.

She must have whimpered.

"Shh," he soothed, rubbing her back. "It's over."

She got a hold of herself. Control came back by slow degrees. And with it came pride, fanning out like the gloriously preening tail feathers on the peacock that strutted through the barn.

She drew back, took a breath, looked into Wyatt's concerned eyes. "I killed that snake."

"Yeah." His voice wasn't all that steady. "Killed it dead."

She gave a nervous laugh. "Made a heck of a mess is what I did. And that's a mess I'm *not* cleaning up."

He cupped her chin and tilted her face up, pressing his lips to hers in one of those soul-stirring kisses that she could spend all day tasting. "I'll take care of it," he said softly. "And thank you."

Emotions she couldn't define swam in his eyes. He still kept so much locked away.

"You're welcome."

"Want to keep the skin? Make a pair of boots?"

A shudder skipped up her spine. "No thank you. I don't want anything that has to do with snakes anywhere close to me and the ones I love."

He went very still. She'd included him as one she loved. Oh, she hadn't spelled it out, but she didn't have to. It was so obvious. She'd been careful not to say it aloud, not to put pressure, although every time they made love the words were like an ache in her throat.

With the aftermath of pumped-up courage over killing the snake, she wasn't going to take back her words. They were her feelings. She owned them. He could do with them what he wanted.

She put her hand against the side of his firm jaw, raised up and lightly kissed his lips. Then left him standing looking after her as she went to count the chickens.

As long as she was here, she wanted to make sure any fowl they ate came from the market, not from her henhouse.

THE HOUSE GLEAMED, the animals were fed and a casserole was assembled and in the fridge ready to go in the oven. The extra casserole was in a covered dish.

"Come on, Ian. Let's go to town. And no, you can't take the dogs." Lady and Ian both whined. Thank goodness Chinook was with Wyatt today, or he'd have probably complained, too.

Honestly, kid and animals were ganging up on her. And darned if she didn't love it.

She loaded her truck and paused when she saw Wyatt mounted on Tornado, riding out of the corral.

As always, there seemed to be a radar between them. He turned, saw her and doubled back.

He looked so tall and sexy sitting atop the horse. The saddle creaked as he leaned an elbow on the horn, a rope loosely held in his gloved hands.

"I'm going into town to help Iris out at the saloon for a while."

"You've handled a pretty full load already this morning. You're not overdoing things, are you?"

"No. I'm fine. Truly," she said when he just frowned at her. "Besides, we're meeting to organize a fund-raiser for the fire department."

His lips twitched. "Want my wallet now or later?"

She laughed. "Later will be fine." She started to get in the car.

"Hannah?"

"Yes?"

"Plan good. I happen to be part of that volunteer fire department."

As he would be, she thought. He was firmly entrenched in this community, had a stake in every aspect of it, from the land to the people.

That was one of the things she loved about him.

She reversed out of the dirt drive and followed the dusty trail to the road. The air through the open window smelled of grass, sunshine and cattle. It made her heart speed up a little faster.

When she passed the two white crosses on the side of the road that marked where Becky and Timmy had died, her heart pumped even harder. But in sadness this time.

"I want to take care of him for you," she whispered.

THE DIAGONAL SPACES in front of Brewer's Saloon were unusually full for this time of day and Hannah was glad she'd come. Iris and Lloyd would need the extra help.

She gathered up her dish and Ian and went inside, the smell of onions and charbroiled burgers vying with the faint smell of cigar smoke and beer.

Once again her gaze was drawn to the sign over the bar proclaiming it a family establishment. In her old life, she'd never have thought to go into a bar alone, or even a restaurant for that matter.

And she wouldn't have been greeted with hugs, waves and friendly calls. Everyone knew her name here and genuinely cared about her.

They also knew Wyatt and his land and they knew more about his business than he probably did. If one of them got sick, a neighbor would be able to walk right in the ranch house and take over the kitchen, see to the livestock, pitch in without having to ask a single question.

And they wouldn't ask for a single thing in return, either.

"Here, hon, let me take that dish," Iris said, giving both Ian and Hannah a quick kiss. "It'll be a while before we can do any planning for the fund-raiser. Lord, just when I think the crowd in here's gonna thin out, another wave comes in. Ozzie and his cronies—my husband included—have gone a bit overboard."

"They didn't expect quite such a stampede of women?"

"No. And it's wearing me out."

"Well, you've got another pair of willing hands. I'll take those tables." She pointed to the left. "You catch whatever Maedean's not getting."

"Bless you. I didn't mean for you to come in and work."

"I'm delighted to do it."

"Don't lift anything too heavy, now. The cord'll wrap around the baby's neck."

Hannah gave her a look. "That's an old wives tale and you know it."

With Ian happily pressed into service passing out menus and chattering with the customers, Hannah worked alongside Iris and Maedean. She'd never waitressed before and gained a new appreciation for the servers. The blisters on her palms stung as she gripped trays and icy glasses of water, tea and soda.

The customers were accommodating and helped out by bussing tables on their way out or going to the kitchen to retrieve their own meals.

The lunch hour ended up more like a community meal rather than a restaurant service. Someone played a lively tune on the jukebox and several folks did an impromptu sing-along with Aretha Franklin as she lamented about respect.

It was festive, exhausting and wonderful.

Collapsing at the bar an hour later, Hannah watched Iris make her way in that direction.

"Well," Iris said. "I'll have to put you on the payroll."

"Don't be silly. I've had a ball."

"Oh, darlin' you are an angel sent right from above."

Hannah linked hands with Iris. "I think it's you all who are my angels. I feel...I don't know if I can put it into words. I love it here. It's exactly where I want to be, what I want...." Her words trailed off.

Iris squeezed her fingers. "Are wedding vows scheduled for any time soon?"

Hannah's heart sank. She shook her head.

"Oh, hon, you haven't given up hope, have you?"

"No." She felt odd discussing the subject with Iris, Becky's mother, but knew that the woman was someone she could trust. "Did you know Wyatt feels responsible for the accident?"

Iris sucked in a breath. Her eyes turned sad. "That's plain ridiculous. No one blames Wyatt."

"Oh, I think he knows that. But he blames himself."

Releasing Hannah's hands, Iris shot her husband a look that clearly told him to find something to do farther down the bar.

Looking annoyed, he took his polishing rag and glasses and retreated, giving them privacy.

"My Becky was restless. It had been growing for a while, even when she was a girl. Then Wyatt courted her and in the new blush of love, she had something and someone to beat back the yearning. She convinced herself he could fill her up. By the time the restless spirits started creeping back, she was pregnant with Timmy. She had a new purpose, something to keep her mind off the specter that kept rising inside her." Iris sat back on the bar stool, smoothed her apron.

"After Timmy was born, the responsibility of the baby occupied her time. And Wyatt doted on them—Timmy was his heart. But once again it wasn't enough for Becky. It was as though she were always running one step ahead of depression. I didn't know how to help her."

"Oh, Iris." There was so little Hannah could say.

"I know." With a gentle smile, Iris silently thanked Hannah for the compassion. "Right before Becky left that last time, she told me she didn't want Timmy to grow up to be a rancher, no matter what the size of his inheritance. She wanted him to be a lawyer or computer tycoon or something. And she wanted someone like that for herself."

Hannah shook her head sadly. "I was married to a lawyer. He was just as tied to his job as a dedicated rancher is to his land. But Allan didn't have the moral code or depth that Wyatt has. Allan didn't have time for us—so I know plenty about loneliness. He didn't pay attention to Ian or me. Sometimes I wonder if Ian would even recognize his father if he were to pass him on the street."

"That's awful."

"I've had life that offers 'more'—the parties and culture and plastic, shallow people. I don't mean to sound ugly, but that's the type of crowd Allan hung out with. I know it's what I *don't* want."

"You're stronger inside than Becky."

"Oh, no."

"I'm not comparing. I loved my daughter. She had

wonderful qualities, and I'll miss her horribly for the rest of my life. But you, Hannah, are indeed a strong woman. You're dedicated to your children, to people. It radiates from you.''

''Wyatt doesn't seem to think I'll stick.''

''Wyatt's not looking past his nose.''

Hannah smiled gently. ''My husband didn't love me.''

''Oh, honey.''

''It's true. I've accepted it. I've grown, though, and I know who I am now. I know I need to be loved.''

''I understand that. Wyatt has the capacity to love deeply.''

''But does he have the desire? If he can't, I can't stay.''

''Oh, I don't even want to think about losing you. You won't leave, will you?''

''I'd planned to go to my sister's in Billings if Wyatt and I didn't suit. But plans have changed. Tori's living in Alaska now. I haven't told Wyatt yet. He still thinks I have someplace to go.''

''You can come to us,'' Iris said resolutely. ''Lloyd and I have room. In fact, that might not be a bad idea now that I think about it. Wyatt was supposed to offer you marriage—''

''*He* didn't know that.''

''That's beside the point. Perhaps he needs a push. You and Ian are welcome in our home any time, for as long as you want. If you want to put a little distance between the two of you, you come to us.''

''I appreciate the offer. And I'll give it some thought.''

Vera Tillis joined them at the bar, armed with a list of ideas for the firemen's fund-raiser. Together the women organized and planned right down to the last potato sack race and scheduled the to-do for a week from Sunday.

Hannah hoped she'd still be here.

As Hannah said her goodbyes and strapped Ian in the truck, she thought about Iris's offer. She'd been here nearly a month. Was she kidding herself when she thought she saw more in Wyatt's eyes? Was she placing more importance in his touch? Reading more into the reverent way he sketched her skin with his fingertips, held her so tenderly, kissed her pregnant tummy as though it were *his* baby growing in her womb?

She wanted to believe all those little things would add up to a whole. Would add up to love.

But he hadn't given her the words.

And because she wanted so badly to hear those words, was she perhaps assuming too much? Assigning feelings to him that weren't actually there?

The eternal optimist in her said that wasn't the case. Even Iris—who knew Wyatt well—believed he had deep feelings for her. She'd give it a few more days. Because leaving him would break her heart.

She passed a sign proclaiming this cattle country and advising folks to eat beef. She decided she ought to remind Wyatt of that lest he start culling her sweet chickens.

Humming along with the radio, the sweet smell of grass and alfalfa wafting through the open window, she glanced over at Ian. His eyes were getting heavy and he'd be asleep before long.

She looked back at the road and her heart slammed right into her throat, her arms going numb.

A huge antlered animal stood in the middle of the road.

She stomped on the brakes, automatically shot out a hand to brace Ian even though he was belted in.

Tires screamed horribly against blacktop. The truck shuddered as if it were flying apart. Her mouth opened on a scream that never materialized.

An eternity passed in slow motion as the truck kept sliding and sliding and sliding.

Please, oh please, oh please. Stop!

The animal's startled eyes were practically looking through the windshield as she slammed her own eyes shut and braced for impact.

Chapter Fourteen

Wyatt flew over his land, pride filling him as he surveyed all that was his.

"Look at those girls," he murmured. "Not too fat, just healthy and happy." Two heifers stood away from the herd, watching over the calves. Baby-sitting, he mused. They would wait for relief before taking their turn to graze. People didn't realize what great animals cows were.

And thinking of great cattle reminded him of the talk he'd tried to have with Cherry again this morning. For the life of him, he didn't understand her hesitation or her attitude over selling him Casanova. She needed the funds and he needed the bull.

Instead of having a rational business discussion, she'd mouthed some crazy thing about him being wrapped up in his personal life and couldn't see what was plain as day and right in his backyard. She was talking in circles, and frustrated, he'd excused himself.

Females.

The crackling of the radio sent a tingle up his spine.

A ghost walking over your grave, his mother had always said.

"Anybody! Wyatt! Doc!" Trevor's frantic, tinny voice blasting through the speakers sent Wyatt's heart ramming against his chest.

"Oh, man oh, man, it's Hannah's truck." A pause. Calmer now, but not by much. "It's in the ditch."

Wyatt had been looking out over the land. Now his gaze jerked to the highway as he cranked hard on the yoke, the little plane banking sharply, allowing him to survey the road that ran from the ranch into town.

His jaw ached with the force of his clenched teeth. He had to be calm.

Déjà vu swept over him—he tried to beat it back. He wanted to shake his fist, shout and curse.

His hands were absolutely steady, his eyes stinging behind the lenses of his dark glasses.

He saw Trevor's horse running hard.

At the same time, he saw Hannah's green truck tipped on its side in the ditch, the driver's side tires still spinning.

An elk lay dead in the road.

Nausea swamped him. He gripped the mike, cleared his throat, and swept a quick visual over the highway.

"Wyatt here, Trevor. I'm over you. I'm landing. Give me room. And for God's sake, don't touch her."

If she's even alive.

"Cheyenne here, Wyatt," Sheriff Bodine said. "I'm five minutes from the turnoff to your place. I haven't passed her."

"You will in a minute." Even as he concentrated

on the plane's gauges and his air speed, going through
the rote motions of landing, he could hear the wail of
Cheyenne's sirens through the radio as the sheriff
screamed up the highway in his cruiser, advising dis-
patch of his location, pedal no doubt mashed to the
floorboard, never letting up.

The wheels of the plane touched and skidded
against asphalt. Wyatt didn't realize he was praying.
He barely heard the chatter on the radio as cowboys
and neighbors burned up the wires giving their coordinates, judging if they were close enough to help
or if their efforts would be best used in another way.

"This is Chance, Cheyenne." The doctor. Thank
God, Wyatt thought. Most everyone around moni-
tored their neighbor's radio frequency via scanners—
including the sheriff and the doctor. "I've been out
on a house call at the Turmans'. I'm just now inter-
secting with the highway from their service road
which'll put me a few minutes behind you."

"Okay, Doc. We'll wait for you," Cheyenne responded. "Hear that, Wyatt? Take your own advice
and don't move them."

Wyatt didn't hear the rest of the admonishment. He
was already unstrapping himself and leaping from the
plane, running, heart pumping, mind numb, refusing
to think.

The air bag would have deployed, exploding in
Hannah's face... against the baby. And Ian...

"She's okay, boss. They all are," Trevor said.

He didn't believe his friend. His mind wasn't even
calculating what he was seeing.

For an instant everything turned inward. Blood,

trickling down lifeless waxen skin. A tiny baby boy slumped in a car seat.

He blinked. Heard Hannah's voice, the sweet sound of Ian crying.

Oh, God, they were alive. It wasn't Becky and Timmy all over again.

His paralysis lifted. He checked the truck, found it steady, and climbed up to peer through the driver's window. "Sweetheart, don't move."

Her smile was a little tremulous. "I already did."

Sure enough, she was out of her seat belt and sitting on the passenger door, Ian cradled in her lap. She had the hem of her skirt pressed against the boy's forehead.

With the truck tilted like this, she was mashed in pretty tight, but alive. *Alive.*

"Get a rope, Trevor. We've got to get this door open."

Adrenaline pumping, he imagined he could rip the steel off its hinges with his bare hands, but he made himself be patient.

Using Trevor's horse and the rope as a pulley, they were able to pry open the door, giving Wyatt a clear entry to get to Hannah and Ian.

"Why didn't the air bag deploy?"

"I had it disconnected when I bought the truck. With the baby and all, I just didn't trust it."

He nodded and his throat ached. God, he hated this feeling. The pain. The fear. "Be still, okay?"

"Wyatt?" Ian said, his voice sounding small. "C-can you g-get me way up to the sky?"

Oh man. He was going to lose it.

"Sure can, partner." His voice cracked. He cleared his throat, eased himself into the truck through the opening. It was cramped quarters, but he could maneuver.

He could touch them.

And right now, he desperately needed to touch them.

His palm trembled as it passed over Hannah's face, the beginning of a bruise swelling on her cheek.

"I hit that poor moose," Hannah said.

"I know, sweetheart." It was an elk, but he wasn't going to quibble. He glanced up at Trevor and the other man nodded. He would get the animal out of sight so Hannah wouldn't have to see it. "Are you okay? The baby?" His hand shook as it skimmed over her stomach.

"Everything feels okay."

"Doc Hammond's on his way. He'll check and make sure."

"Right now, we'd just like to get out of here. This is even more embarrassing than you getting the truck stuck."

The wildlife nearly killed her and she made jokes. He didn't know whether to laugh or cry.

He focused on Ian.

"Does anything hurt you, sport?" He ran his hands over the boy's legs, arms, neck and back.

Ian shook his head, dislodging Hannah's pressure to his head wound. Blood trickled down his cheek. Wyatt's vision hazed for just an instant, his mind turning inward, to another time, to another bloody scene.

Car doors slammed outside, jerking him back to the present. Hannah and Ian were alive. He had to keep reminding himself of that.

Wyatt looked up, saw both Cheyenne and Chance peer into the car.

"They're both moving around and say nothing's hurting," he reported, surprised that his voice sounded steady and firm. "Ian's got a cut on his head and Hannah has a bruise on her cheek. Think it'll be safe for me to hand them up to you?"

"Keep them as still and straight as you can," Chance said.

Carefully he lifted Ian from Hannah's arms and passed him up through the truck door opening into Chance and Cheyenne's arms. He turned back to Hannah who was already struggling to get her feet under her.

"Wait, sweetheart. Let me have a look at you first."

"I'm fine."

"Humor me." As he'd done with Ian, he ran his hands over her body, their faces so close their breaths mingled. Unable to help himself, he drew her to him, just held on for a long heartbreaking moment, buried his face in her lemony hair.

The ache in his throat throbbed, robbed him of speech and pride. His eyes were damp. "You scared me," he whispered.

"I know," she said just as softly. "I'm sorry."

"Ready, Wyatt?" Cheyenne asked.

"Ready. Let me do the work, Hannah," he said, slipping his arms beneath her. It was awkward, but years of lifting saddles and bales of hay and wrestling cows to the ground gave him the strength to boost her straight up and out of the top of the truck door.

Cheyenne and Trevor were right there to take her from him. As much as he knew he needed the help, he hated to relinquish her, didn't trust anyone else with her.

Vaulting out behind her, he landed on the ground, took her back from the sheriff.

"I've got her now." He didn't want to let go. And those were dangerous thoughts.

He sat down on the ground next to where Chance was checking Ian, and kept Hannah cradled in his lap, his hand resting over the baby in her womb.

"This guy's got a tough noggin," the doctor said. "But he'll be fine. A bit sore, I imagine. I'll check him over again when we get to the house and put a stitch in that cut. No need to go to the hospital."

Chance turned to Hannah, raised a brow when Wyatt didn't appear willing to let her go. With a shrug, he examined her while Wyatt held her, shined a light in her eyes, checked pupils, pulse, took out a stethoscope and listened to the baby's heartbeat.

"Any cramping?"

"No."

The doctor stood, nodded. "I'll take them to your place," he said to Wyatt. "Check them out a bit more, but I think everyone's fine. And very lucky."

"I'll take them," Wyatt said.

Cheyenne raised a brow. "Uh, somebody's got to get this plane off my highway. You see anybody else here with a pilot's license?"

Wyatt swore. For a moment longer, he held Hannah to him, emotions swelling, the power of them almost too much to contain.

He couldn't do this, he realized. The fear was too strong, the pain too excruciating. He was in danger of his heart shattering. He was in too deep.

He'd fooled himself into believing that they could go on like they were, letting one day turn into the next. He'd convinced himself that if he hid from the words, the feelings, he'd never have to face the devil or pay the price.

But the devil had just had the last laugh.

NEIGHBORS STREAMED IN and out of the house for the rest of the day, each bearing food. They'd have enough to eat for the rest of the month.

Hannah kept repeating that she was fine, but folks wanted to see for themselves. Iris fussed over Hannah's bruise, cried over Ian's stitches then simply held Hannah in a fierce hug that had released emotions Hannah had tried her best to keep a lid on. She'd been wishing for her mother, the void feeling so much wider, deeper, fresher. Without words, Iris understood.

The front yard looked like a cattlemen's convention with all the pickups coming and going. No one stayed long. If they'd been needed, they would have.

And even though Wyatt was giving her a wide berth, which confused her, he was still watchful, frowning every time she so much as lifted a teacup.

She'd managed to get everyone out of the house and was about to enjoy a moment to herself, hoping she wouldn't continue to see that poor moose every time she closed her eyes, hoping she wouldn't forever have the echo of squealing tires and the sound of Ian's scream ringing in her ears, when Cherry Peyton stepped through the back door.

Hannah was surprised despite herself. Cherry wasn't the socializing, bring-a-pie type.

"Heard you've had a rough morning," Cherry said.

"Rougher for that moose," Hannah replied, trying to judge the atmosphere, unsure how to proceed with this woman, her closest neighbor. She decided to leave the tone up to Cherry and follow the other woman's cue.

"I'd heard it was an elk."

Hannah shrugged. How could she be expected to accurately recognize or distinguish an animal's breed when it was in the process of becoming a hood ornament? And despite the fact that she wouldn't have known the difference in any case, she refused to feel inferior.

Cherry sighed, sat at the kitchen table. "How are you?"

"Shook up, but fine."

Cherry glanced down at Hannah's stomach. "Wendell and I weren't able to have children. I wanted them terribly, but it wasn't meant to be."

"I'm sorry."

Cherry nodded. "I was a young woman when Wendell died—only thirty-two. I'm forty now, and feeling older by the day. It's getting harder and harder for me to hang on, to the ranch, and…to get past the loneliness. And even though I'm older than Wyatt is,

I've held a flame in my heart that something could work out between us—two grieving people who could heal one another's heart. I resented you when you came here.''

''I know,'' Hannah said softly, honestly. Here was common ground between the two of them, even if it was competition.

''I think I'm past that now, and I'd like to start over as neighbors, if you're interested.''

''I'm interested.''

''You've a generous heart, Hannah Richmond. And you've accomplished what I couldn't. I guess Ozzie and the gang knew what they were doing when they manipulated you into Wyatt's life.''

''I don't know that he's healed, Cherry. He holds so much of himself back.''

''That he does.'' She stood and edged toward the door. ''But he's a hell of a man. I'm pulling for you, Hannah.''

''Uh, Cherry? About that bull—''

''I'm going to sell him to Wyatt.''

''Why don't you just sell him half? Be partners?''

Cherry stopped, frowned. Clearly, the idea hadn't occurred to her.

''I don't know a thing about this sort of transaction or the bull or anything, but if he's so studly, it seems to me he'd have enough—'' she waved her hand, unable to come up with the word ''—uh, stamina to father two herds. You need the capital to give your ranch a boost—if you truly want to hold on to it.''

Cherry nodded. ''I do.''

''And Wyatt said his ancestors had parlayed a single bull and a few heifers into a dynasty," Hannah continued. "I don't know why he can't be a little patient, start out on a smaller scale if need be. That way you both win."

She ducked her head, feeling silly with her long speech. Especially since she didn't know squat about the subject.

"You're absolutely right. I'm an all-or-nothing kind of person. I hadn't thought of sharing."

"Wyatt's pretty much all-or-nothing, too." He'd given his all once and claimed he had nothing more to give now. Relationship wise, that was. As much as she wanted it to be otherwise, those were Wyatt's feelings. She couldn't wave a wand and change him. "For the bull, I think he'll compromise."

WYATT SAT by Ian's bedside. For three days now, he'd avoided the boy, only seeking him out when he knew Ian was asleep or close to it.

"Wyatt?" Ian whispered.

"I'm right here, buddy."

"Nikki said you could be my daddy, cuz Stony's not her really and truly daddy, but she gets to keep him for her daddy." His words were slurred, on the verge of sleep. "Could I keep you?"

Wyatt lifted Ian's small hand, rested his forehead against it. The boy had fallen asleep before he could even answer.

"Oh, Ian, buddy. I don't want to lose you."

Hannah flattened herself against the wall, not wanting Wyatt to see her there. At the sound of Wyatt's raw words, she eased away from Ian's doorway and went to the room next door.

She felt the horrible ache in the back of her throat, the sensation of her nose swelling, running, eyes stinging. She buried her face in the pillow to stop the flow of hot tears drenching her face.

Wyatt had pulled back after the accident, had been avoiding them. When she'd gone back to sleeping in the guest room next to Ian's, he'd looked sad, but he hadn't said a word.

She didn't understand his distance. She wanted to set aside her pride and beg.

Oh, God, it was exactly what she said she wouldn't do. Could she compromise her vow that this time she wouldn't settle for less than a full measure of love?

She loved Wyatt...

And Wyatt loved her kid.

With Ian, he let down his guard. He showed his emotions. With her, he wouldn't.

Could she live like that? She gripped the charm necklace that lay cool and crushing against her chest.

She knew the answer. As much as she loved him, he'd yet to give her the main thing she needed. The words. Love. For her. For who she was, not who anybody expected her to be, or who she might become.

She'd almost forgotten the lesson she'd learned through Allan. Almost believed she could compromise, love enough for both of them...wait for him.

But waiting on love was a thing of the past.

It was time to leave. She would take Iris up on her offer.

HER THROAT WAS RAW, her eyes swollen the next morning as she packed hers and Ian's suitcases. Fat tears dripped down Ian's face as he hugged the puppies.

"No, mom," he whispered. "I don't want to go."

She knelt by his bed, cupped his sweet cheeks in her palms. "I know, honey." She wouldn't cry again, swore there were no tears left. "You have to be strong for Mama now."

He didn't understand. But like the little man he was, he sensed his mother's fragility. The need to be good. "'Kay."

She rose with his hand in hers, and picked up her suitcase.

Wyatt stood in the bedroom doorway, hands fisted at his side. The sight of him jolted her.

"You're leaving, then?"

She nodded. *Ask me to stay.*

He was stoic, his eyes haunted. He took the suitcase from her, held it between them for a long moment.

She thought he would say something. He didn't.

She followed him down the stairs. Skeeter had her rental trailer hooked to one of Wyatt's trucks. She'd asked him to do it for her.

She watched as Wyatt bent down to Ian, as her son wrapped his little arms around Wyatt's neck and held on, tears rolling down his cheeks.

"Bye," Ian whispered, so solemn it nearly broke her heart.

Wyatt tipped his head, pulled his hat down lower on his brow as Ian climbed up into the truck.

Hannah stood next to him. She'd told herself she wouldn't burden him with the words. To hell with it.

"I love you, you know."

The agony that flashed in his eyes was horrible to witness. He was a man on the edge, but it was *he* who would have to step off the cliff, to take a chance.

She cupped his cheek, wanting to say more, knowing she couldn't. In the end, she simply pressed a soft kiss to his lips and got in the truck. Her eyes were dry until she started the engine.

Wyatt ached, felt like his insides were ripping apart. He longed to reach out to her, to stop her. His heart pounded, yet his feet wouldn't move. His voice wouldn't work.

I love you, you know.

Oh, God, oh, God, oh, God. The violent refrain echoed in his brain. A prayer. A plea.

The ranch hands were lined up at the fence—their expressions somber and accusing. They took off their hats as Hannah slowly drove by.

Wyatt's vision blurred. Ridiculous.

Skeeter made a disgusted sound. "You gonna just let her get away? She's the best thing that's ever happened to you."

He still didn't speak. Something sparkled in the sun.

He looked closer.

Hanging on the porch rail was the crystal heart Hannah had always worn—she'd never been without it. It was the necklace her Aunt Shirley had given her. To Hannah that necklace represented family...and love.

And she'd left her heart right here on his doorstep.

Oh, God. Wyatt realized that they *were* a family. He'd convinced himself that love hurt.

He now realized that it hurt much worse *not* to love.

She'd killed a snake for him—faced her worse fear. So, why couldn't he do the same for her? Let go of the fear?

"No, by God, I'm not going to let her get away."

"Hot damn!" Skeeter whooped.

Tornado was ground-tied a few feet away. Wyatt vaulted onto the horse and tore off after her.

It didn't take much to catch her. She'd been traveling at a snail's pace and she'd already stopped.

Wyatt's heart tumbled when he saw Ian bouncing in his seat, his tiny white teeth gleaming, his arm waving.

The cowboys lined along the fence started cheering.

Hannah heard the whooping and carrying on. She sniffed, tried to clear the tears that blinded, that had forced her to stop. "What in the world?"

Stunned, she looked in the rearview mirror, saw the dust. Saw Wyatt racing on his horse after her.

Her heart somersaulted in her chest. She put the truck in park, opened the door and got out.

With her hand shading her eyes, she waited, felt the butterfly wings of elation and fragile hope flutter in her stomach.

Wyatt reined in beside her, leaped off his horse.

His throat was dry and his heart was racing. "I love

you, too." They were the hardest words he'd said in over four years.

He snatched her to him, lifted her right up off the ground, pressed his lips to hers, and kissed her until he couldn't breathe.

"I love you." Easier this time. "Don't go. You came here looking for a family. Be my family, Hannah. Please. You and Ian and our baby girl."

"Oh, Wyatt."

"I've got to take a chance."

"There still aren't any guarantees."

"I don't need them." And he found that the words were true. He'd almost lost her. "It doesn't matter. I know you love me. I've known it all along, but I was too damn scared of losing, of hurting like that again. But if I only have one day with you or a hundred years, it doesn't matter. I'll cherish every second of each day."

Life was too short. She touched the deepest, most tender corner of his heart. And the feeling kept growing, spreading to encompass all of him.

"You make me whole, Hannah." His voice was deep and soft and raw with emotion. "I love you. And I love your kids—*our* kids," he corrected. "Ian and this baby girl."

When he put his hand over her stomach, Hannah's heart flooded with joy.

Oh, Mama and Aunt Shirley. Are you watching?

"Marry me, Hannah. Let me give you and these children my name, my life...my love."

"Yes."

"I'm serious. I want to adopt these kids."

"Yes."

Joy swelled in him. He laughed and kissed her, twirled her around, charmed by the dazed look of elation on her beautiful face, by the single-syllable answers.

The cowboys cheered. Ian bounced in his seat, mimicking the approval. The baby between them kicked and tumbled, adding her blessings, too.

Hannah, her heart bursting, knew that she was home at last. She'd found herself. And she'd found her cowboy.

Ozzie and his buddies would get their wish—another woman in Shotgun Ridge—and babies.

And if Hannah had her way, she would give her Montana cowboy many more babies in the years to come.

"Ladies and Gentlemen, we've got a treat for sure," Lloyd Brewer extolled, his voice booming through the microphone. "This here's our major beef—not to disparage any of our other fine bachelors, mind you."

Major beef? For the love of God, Ethan felt his face heat with the flush of embarrassment.

"Our next and final bachelor up for bid is Ethan Callahan. A fine catch, I'm telling you. A renowned horse breeder residing right here in Shotgun Ridge. If it's a fancy five-star dinner in a swanky city you've a hankering for, or a hike through Yellowstone, this man has the means to make your dreams come true. He'll fly you there in his own personal airplane, or squire you in one of his flashy cars—though I'm sure there's a sin somewhere in owning more than one pleasure vehicle," Lloyd added dryly.

Hoots and hollers ensued, and it was just the thing to relax Ethan. He was extremely proud of every one of his toys, from the Vette to the chopper. And if Lloyd teasingly hinted that it was gluttony to own three cars as well as all the other stuff, so be it. Pastor

Lucas would just have to pray harder over Ethan's soul.

Because Ethan was a man who loved to have fun. And from the sound and enthusiasm of this crowd, they were definitely festive and out for a good time.

Okay, he thought, grinning and winking at a brunette in gold sequins. I can get into this.

Unbuttoning his tuxedo jacket, he slid a hand in one pocket of his trousers and poured on the charm, working the crowd of women whose hands were raising faster than Lloyd could ask for a bid or raise the amount.

His grin widened and he scanned the room. He had to hand it to the old folks. They knew how to pack a room and they threw a heck of a party. The place was filled with glittering, sweet-smelling ladies. At this rate, the town balance was likely to tip in the opposite direction—too many women and not enough cowboys. He kind of liked the sound of that.

Competitive spirit and ego reared up as he worked the room with his eyes, enticing women to up their bids. If he had to be a part of this crazy plan, he might as well turn it into a challenge, make sure he commanded a higher price than his neighbors or employees.

His gaze swept past the door, then slammed back, causing him to stop his performance midstride.

Oh, man, he thought when his brain finally kicked back in gear. *Here comes trouble in a tight pair of jeans.*

As though he'd spoken the thought aloud, her gaze honed in on his, held.

And for an instant, Ethan forgot to draw a breath.

She was a dynamite package, self-assured, holding his stare when most women would have coyly looked away. That alone intrigued him…and turned him on.

He raised a brow. An invitation.

She appeared to struggle with a reluctant smile, then shifted her attention, only pausing for a bare instant as she noted the dressy attire in the rest of the room versus her casual sweater and jeans. With a nearly imperceptible shrug, she gave her head a gentle shake, flicked her honey-blond hair off her shoulders, and strolled into the room as though she wore a sexy floor-length silk gown and diamonds. With a smile, she let Ozzie Peyton direct her to an empty seat. Right up front.

Mmm, yes indeed, Ethan thought, following her progress with his eyes, his gaze riveted on the sassy sway of her hips in those skintight jeans. *Mighty fine.*

Suddenly the evening took on a new energy.

But he was falling down on his performance. He was supposed to flirt with *all* the women. Even though he'd already set his sights on just the one.

HARLEQUIN HOME FOR THE HOLIDAYS CONTEST 9119
OFFICIAL RULES
NO PURCHASE NECESSARY TO ENTER

1. To enter, follow directions published in the offer to which you are responding. Contest begins April 1, 2000 and ends on July 31, 2000. Method of entry may vary. Mailed entries must be postmarked by July 31, 2000 and received by August 7, 2000.

2. Contest entry may be, at times, presented via the Internet but will be restricted solely to residents of certain geographic areas that are disclosed on the Web site. To enter via the Internet, if permissible, access the Harlequin romance Web site (http://www.eHarlequin.com) and follow the directions displayed online. Online entries must be received by 11:59 p.m. E.S.T on July 31, 2000.

   In lieu of submitting an entry online, enter by mail by hand-printing (or typing) on an 8" x 11" plain piece of paper, your name, address (including zip code), contest number/name, and in 250 words or fewer, tell us why you would like to go home for the Thanksgiving or Christmas holiday. Mail via first-class mail to: Harlequin Home for the Holidays Contest 9119, (in the U.S.) P.O. Box 9069, Buffalo, NY 14269-9069, (in Canada) P.O. Box 637, Fort Erie, Ontario, Canada L2A 5X3.

   Limit one entry per person, household address and e-mail address. Online and/or mailed entries received from persons residing in geographic areas in which Internet entry is not permissible will be disqualified.

3. Essays will be judged by a panel of members of the Harlequin editorial and marketing staff based on the following criteria:
   Sincerity—40%
   Originality and Creativity—35%
   Emotionally Compelling—25%
   In the event of a tie, duplicate prizes will be awarded. Decisions of the judges are final.

4. All entries become the property of Torstar Corp. and will not be returned. No responsibility is assumed for lost, late, illegible, incomplete, inaccurate, nondelivered or misdirected mail or misdirected e-mail, for technical, hardware or software failures of any kind, lost or unavailable network connections, or failed, incomplete, garbled or delayed computer transmission or any human error that may occur in the receipt or processing of the entries in this contest.

5. Contest open only to residents of the U.S. (except Puerto Rico) and Canada, who are 18 years of age or older, and is void wherever prohibited by law; all applicable laws and regulations apply. Any litigation within the Province of Québec respecting the conduct or organization of a publicity contest may be submitted to the Régie des alcools, des courses et des jeux for a ruling. Any litigation respecting the award of a prize may be submitted to the Régie des alcools, des courses et des jeux only for the purpose of helping the parties reach a settlement. Employees and immediate family members of Torstar Corp. and D.L. Blair, Inc., their affiliates, subsidiaries and all other agencies, entities and persons connected with the use, marketing or conduct of this contest are not eligible to enter. Taxes on prizes are the sole responsibility of winners. Acceptance of any prize offered constitutes permission to use winner's name, photograph or other likeness for the purposes of advertising, trade and promotion on behalf of Torstar Corp., its affiliates and subsidiaries without further compensation to the winner, unless prohibited by law.

6. Winners will be determined no later than August 31, 2000, and will be notified by mail. Winners will be required to sign and return an Affidavit of Eligibility form within 15 days after winner notification. Noncompliance within that time period may result in disqualification and an alternate winner may be selected. Winners of trip must execute a Release of Liability prior to ticketing and must possess required travel documents (e.g. passport, photo ID) where applicable. Trip must be taken on dates specified by sponsor. No substitution of prize permitted by winner. Torstar Corp. and D.L. Blair, Inc., their parents, affiliates and subsidiaries are not responsible for errors in printing or electronic presentation of contest, entries and/or game pieces. In the event of printing or other errors, which may result in unintended prize values or duplication of prizes, all affected game pieces or entries shall be null and void. If for any reason the Internet portion of the contest is not capable of running as planned, including infection by computer virus, bugs, tampering, unauthorized intervention, fraud, technical failures or any other causes beyond the control of Torstar Corp. which corrupt or affect the administration, secrecy, fairness, integrity or proper conduct of the contest, Torstar Corp. reserves the right, at its sole discretion, to disqualify any individual who tampers with the entry process and to cancel, terminate, modify or suspend the contest or the Internet portion thereof. In the event of a dispute regarding an online entry, the entry will be deemed submitted by the authorized holder of the e-mail account submitted at the time of entry. Authorized account holder is defined as the natural person who is assigned to an e-mail address by an Internet access provider, online service provider or other organization that is responsible for arranging e-mail address for the domain associated with the submitted e-mail address. Purchase or acceptance of a product offer does not improve your chances of winning.

7. Prizes: (2) Two Grand Prizes—(1) One ticket for round-trip coach air transportation to winner's choice destination to go home for either this Thanksgiving or Christmas holiday from gateway airport nearest winner's home, including round-trip ground transportation to/from airport (approximate value: $3,500 ea.); (5) Five First Prizes—$100 long distance gift certificates. Limit one prize per person. All prizes are valued in U.S. currency.

8. For a list of winners (available after September 29, 2000), send a self-addressed, stamped envelope to: Harlequin Home for the Holidays Contest 9119 Winners, P.O. Box 4200 Blair, NE 68009-4200.

   Contest sponsored by Torstar Corp., P.O. Box 9042, Buffalo, NY 14269-9042.

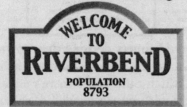

You are now entering

WELCOME TO RIVERBEND
POPULATION 8793

Riverbend…the kind of place where everyone knows your name—and your business. Riverbend…home of the River Rats—a group of small-town sons and daughters who've been friends since high school.

The Rats are all grown up now. Living their lives and learning that some days are good and some days aren't—and that you can get through anything as long as you have your friends.

Starting in July 2000, Harlequin Superromance brings you Riverbend—six books about the River Rats and the Midwest town they live in.

BIRTHRIGHT by **Judith Arnold** (July 2000)
THAT SUMMER THING by **Pamela Bauer** (August 2000)
HOMECOMING by **Laura Abbot** (September 2000)
LAST-MINUTE MARRIAGE by **Marisa Carroll** (October 2000)
A CHRISTMAS LEGACY by **Kathryn Shay** (November 2000)

Available wherever Harlequin books are sold.

Makes any time special™